DARK SUMMER

S. J. COLES

Dark Summer
ISBN # 978-1-83943-731-1
©Copyright S. J. Coles 2021
Cover Art by Erin Dameron-Hill ©Copyright July 2021
Interior text design by Claire Siemaszkiewicz
Pride Publishing

Pride Publishing books by S. J. Coles

Single Books
Blood Winter
Dark Summer
Straight to the Heart

Collections
My Bloody Valentine: Blood Red Roses
Sun, Sea and Small-Town Secrets

DARK SUMMER

Dedication

For Hannah B.

Chapter One

The sun was warm on my face. The brisk wind brought with it the smells of sun-drenched heather and dry grass. The sky was a shade of blue so bright that it almost hurt to look at it. Summer was spreading through the mountains like molten gold, enhancing the colors and the smells, sinking into my flesh and heating my blood. The wind picked up as I reached the ridge and the sweat cooled on my face.

I stood for a moment, breathing deep, and had to admit that I missed sunshine. I'd kept haemophile hours for so long that I hadn't even realized summer had come to the Cairngorms. But despite being out in the sun's heat for the first time in months, the vague chill under my skin didn't dissipate.

I rubbed a hand over my face and made myself take in the view. The undulating mountains, green glens and glistening jewels of the lochs always made me feel like I was standing alone on the face of heaven. Glenroe perched on its rocky outcrop below, the gray stone dark, even in the midday sun, like it couldn't quite let go of its shadows. Scaffolding was bright against the dark stone, and even at this height, I could hear the shouts, clangs and rumbles of the dozens of contractors in the final stages of restoration work. It had taken almost two years and more money than I had ever dreamed, but the sixteenth-century hall was now, finally, almost up to twenty-first-century living standards. The new roof still looked odd to me, accustomed as I was to the gaping holes and worn tarpaulin patch jobs I'd grown up with. But the novelty of not having to share the house with the unpredictable Scottish elements had not yet worn off.

But Terje was gone...again. It had been almost a month this time, the longest he'd ever been away. And my doubts had now permeated me almost to the bone.

I'd made myself accept, right at the start, that there were things I would never be able to understand about my haemophile lover. I was now well-practiced at steering my thoughts away from the industrial refrigeration unit behind a locked door in the cellar, stocked with a mysteriously replenished supply of bottled human blood. And Terje had always gone to great pains to explain that he wouldn't always be around — that, sometimes, he would need to be alone. I told myself that I had accepted that too, and as much as the huge master bed and the high-ceilinged rooms of Glenroe were achingly empty when he was gone, his return was always so full of wonder and pleasure that I soon forgot the strain of his absence.

I'd never met anyone who could absorb my turns of mood like Terje. If I was riled, he let me rant until I ran out of steam, gently questioning to better understand me then offering an insight that either validated or completely deflated my anger. Other times, if there was nothing to be said, he would take my hand and kiss me gently, letting me know without words that it would all be okay, even if he couldn't tell me how.

As the weeks had turned into months, I'd found my habitual fire easing to a warm, steady glow that was oddly pleasant but so unfamiliar that I didn't entirely trust it.

We would walk in the mountains by moonlight and Terje would talk about the places he'd been, the things he'd seen. He talked about the mountains of Norway — the peaks, the caves, the rivers and the ice-bound lakes. He said the Cairngorms were a gentler land, raw and wild but rolling and tranquil, the landscape welcoming, the weather more forgiving.

He said I was like the mountains I'd been born in, that I held the same mysteries and beauty, the same potential for both adventure and danger. For the first time in my life, I had started to entertain the idea that maybe I had the capacity to be happy.

Though I also knew there were parts of him I could never reach and, sometimes, he vanished without warning for days on end. But I had endured this, told myself I'd accepted it. But he'd never been away for more than a fortnight before.

We had our final meeting with the architects restoring Glenroe in Edinburgh the next day. I'd booked a room at a haemophile-friendly hotel. We were supposed to be making a holiday of it — a chance to spend time together in a city we both adored, to make love in a new bed and enjoy a change of scene. Now it looked like I would be going alone.

I shook away the gloomy thoughts, knowing from bitter experience that brooding wouldn't bring him back any quicker, and started back down the mountain, mentally scanning the contents of the new wine cellar. There were several new acquisitions I'd been looking forward to trying, hoping they might taste enough like Terje's Blood to suppress the craving.

The thought sent a finger of ice up my spine.

My uneasiness changed as I approached the house. The machine noise had died. The men who had been tasked with dismantling the scaffolding were clustered together, exchanging words in low voices. Other men were darting between the demountable field office and the open front door of the hall. As I approached, McGregor, the site manager, came out of the office in rock-climbing gear.

"What's going on?"

"Got a man missing," the red-bearded man grumbled in his thick Glaswegian accent. "He went to check on the foundation work and didn't come back."

I blanched. "He went into the caves alone?"

"Sounds like it, the silly sod," McGregor grumbled, shooting a look at a pale-faced man in a helmet and sweat-soaked T-shirt.

"Doug thought he'd better eyeball the foundations before we take the west wing scaffolding down," the man said. "It was supposed to be a quick check…two minutes tops."

"No one's supposed to go down there alone," McGregor said. "Ye all know the score… MacCarthy, what're you playing at?" I was already hurrying inside. "MacCarthy" — McGregor dogged my footsteps — "ye better not be — "

"I know those caves," I insisted, grabbing climbing gloves and a head torch from the racks next to the cellar door.

"You're a civilian," McGregor argued. "Let the rescue team—"

"They're *my* caves," I said. "And you aren't supposed to be down there, anyway. I'm going. I'll be quicker."

McGregor started to protest further, but I was already opening the door, noting with a flare of anger that the keypad had been set to 'unlocked', then racing down the stairs. The door at the bottom was wedged open with a toolbox, and the lights in Terje's apartment were all on. The sleeping cell and industrial fridges were both still locked, but I couldn't stop a surge of anxiety.

By the time I reached the bottom of the second, longer flight of stairs, it was pitch black. The air smelled like stillness and rock. I flicked on the head torch and the echoing emptiness of the Gateway sprang into existence. This high, dry cavern had been cleared of debris hundreds of years before and had been used for everything from sheltering Catholic priests to smuggling illicit whiskey. The rock arched overhead in a series of sharp, black shoulders and the walls were scratched with generations of sacred marks and not-so-sacred graffiti. I hurried past all this to the narrow, black fissure in the wall.

The fissure had been artificially widened at some point in the distant past for some unguessable reason and was the last mark man had made on the Glenroe caverns. It was just wide enough for me to pass through stooped, then I was standing on the lip of a sheer cliff that disappeared into blackness below.

I held my breath and listened. All was silent.

"MacCarthy, you mad bastard," McGregor grumbled, squeezing through after me, his voice echoing in the cavernous chamber, "get yerself back here or so help me—"

"What's the man's name?"

"Doug. Doug Bliss. But we should wait—"

"*Bliss?*" I called, pitching my voice to carry. The sound bounced off the walls and ceiling then faded away. I called again, then once more. After the third echo faded to nothing, I heard a very faint, plaintive call, so weak that the echo barely reached us.

"That's him," McGregor said. "Jesus, Mary and Joseph... Where's the daft prick got to?"

"He's somewhere in the east cave system," I said, scrambling over the edge. "I'll go find him. When the rescue team get here, have them set up ropes and ladders here."

"I still think—"

"It would take them hours to get to him," I cut in as I started to climb, finding the foot and handholds with practiced ease. "I want everyone out of here quickly. Just do as I say."

McGregor's muttered reply was lost in the echo of my boots scraping rock. My arms started to burn, a feeling I hadn't had since my last real climb, years ago. I allowed myself a moment enjoying the pleasant memories it stirred. But then I remembered David Carlisle had been with me and hurriedly shook the thoughts away.

Soon my boots connected with a boulder slide. I scrambled to more level ground then began the arduous clamber across the slanting chamber. Dripping water echoed somewhere to the right. I heaved myself over a rockfall and took a moment to catch my breath. I wasn't as fit as I used to be, and a stitch was starting in my side.

Bliss' pained cries were louder now. I stamped down another flare of anger. The man had just risked his own life climbing down this far, and I couldn't think of a single legitimate reason for him doing so. The events of Blood Winter were now almost two years past, but the memory of Jon Ogdell's, and other corporations' before his, desperation to get ownership of this cave system still made my distrust flare. I climbed on, knowing that the sooner this was over, the sooner I could get the strangers out of Terje's apartment.

Graeme Byrnes Architects were a haemo-friendly company, recommended personally by Ivor Novák, the haemophiles' head lobbyist and parliamentary representative. They'd installed the apartment, complete with a lightproof sleeping cell and fridges, no questions asked. But the need for Terje's survival of Blood Winter to remain secret was imperative, and despite Novák's assurances, I didn't want anyone poking around anymore than they had to.

I could hear Bliss clearly now. I stretched, preparing to tackle the last scramble, but froze with my hands on the rock. I strained my ears, resisting the urge to shush the whimpering man, trying to decide if I had heard the scrape of something solid moving across the rock overhead. But that was impossible… Those chambers were only accessible with ropes. I'd done it once before, against my father's express orders, mainly because he'd told me not to. It had been exhilarating, and the cave beyond, known as the Ballroom, was a thing of such ragged, wild and dangerous beauty that I had been dumbstruck and dreamed about revisiting it many times. But my father had confiscated my rock-climbing gear directly after I'd returned, and by the time he was dead, I'd lost interest in the sport—along with a lot of other things.

No one had laid eyes on the Ballroom since.

I stood, listening, holding my breath, but there was only me, Bliss' labored breathing and the vast, cold silence.

I clambered on. Finally, I spotted the contractor, propped at an awkward angle against a boulder. He squinted up into my light and his expression flattened with relief. He tried to raise an arm but grimaced and clutched his ribs.

"Bliss?" I said, dropping down next to him.

The man nodded, his face screwed up with pain. "Thank Christ," he panted.

"You hurt?"

He nodded, wincing. "Think…think I busted a rib. That's…that's why I couldn't shout."

"What the hell were you doing down here?"

The man's face shifted under its coating of dirt. "Checking…foundations…"

"The foundations are under the house," I muttered, kneeling and checking his legs for broken bones.

"Thought…thought I heard…something."

A prickle went up my spine. "What?"

The man shook his head. "Someone moving around. Thought someone was stuck…wanted to check…" He made a pained noise and I let out an impatient one.

"Okay, okay. Stop trying to speak. Can you stand?"

The man took a couple of moments to catch his breath then tried to get his feet under him. I took hold of the arm opposite the injured ribs and, slowly, he stood. He paled under his coating of dirt.

"Broken rib all right," I said. "Maybe two. Not bloody surprised. This climb's tricky if you don't know where to put your feet."

Bliss nodded. "Yeah, I was fucking dumb. But…but I swear there was someone…"

"Stop talking," I said, not acknowledging the crawling sensation across my skin. "We need to get you as close to the entrance as we can for the rescue team. You ready?"

Bliss set his jaw and nodded. I steadied my footing then pulled the man's arm over my shoulders, dug my foot into the first foothold and eased us up.

It was a slow, painful and sweaty scramble, taking over twice as long as the journey in. Bliss was a capable climber and used his feet and legs well, but with one arm over my shoulders and the other clutching his hurt side, it was awkward and labored, and we had to stop frequently for him to catch his breath. By the time we were within sight of the cliff, I was sweating and aching—and not in a way that generated pleasant memories.

Four Mountain Rescue volunteers were ready with ropes and a stretcher. They hurried forward to take charge of Bliss. I spent the time it took to strap him to a stretcher scanning the caves and listening, but nothing moved or made a sound.

I followed the rescue team back into the house, locking all the doors as I went and making a mental note to change the codes. Bliss was loaded into an ambulance as his colleagues watched in grim silence.

I breathed a sigh of relief and was just about to make my way to the workshop when McGregor, having seen Bliss safely on his way, stopped me. His forehead was tightly furrowed. When he spoke, his voice was low.

"Bliss says he heard someone down there."

"He's mistaken."

McGregor frowned harder. "He seems pretty sure."

"There's no access apart from through the house."

"For a human, maybe."

I kept my face blank. McGregor lowered his voice further. "We've installed apartments like yours for lots of clients. It's our job. But it's my contractual obligation to remind ye of the law against harboring unregistered haemophiles."

I took a moment to ensure my voice was steady before speaking. "We provided you with all the registration documentation before the work started."

"Aye, that I know — or we wouldn't be here. So why is your friend roaming the caves during the day instead of secured in the cell?"

"The resident of the cellar is currently away. But his whereabouts are, frankly, none of your business."

McGregor's lined face shifted. "We'll leave it there then, sir. You understand it's my job to check."

"I understand. Now, if you don't mind, I have my own work to do."

I felt McGregor's eyes on me all the way down the hill.

Clem straightened with a wince from the engine of a ruby-red 1972 VW Beetle at the sound of the workshop door.

"Didn't think I'd see you today," Clem said as I pulled on overalls and a mask.

"Thought I'd get ahead on the Triumph," I said, grabbing the sander and making for the silver Triumph Herald, the only other car in the workshop.

"Phone's been buzzing."

I paused. Clem was wiping his hands on a rag and glaring at the Beetle engine like it had just insulted his mother. I retrieved my phone from where it was sitting on the workshop windowsill.

"This fancy company not sorting a new phone mast?" Clem grumbled as I brushed the thin layer of dust off the phone screen.

"I thought you liked being out of phone range?" I said, noting three emails, two text messages and a missed call notification.

"Aye. But it's distracting, having that thing buzzing away in here all the time."

"I've had all of four calls all year."

"Yeah…and most of them today."

My throat tightened. The emails, missed call and one of the text messages were all from Ivor Novák.

The written messages all said the same thing.

Lord Aviemore,

I would appreciate you getting in touch as soon as possible. There are matters of some importance I wish to discuss.

Yours,

Ivor

This was the third time the haemophile spokesperson had tried to make contact in the last six months but, despite everything he had done for me and Terje, I had never returned his calls. Novák had allowed us to build a life together, facilitating a blood supply and fake registration documents for Terje, but I'd suspected it was more for his benefit than ours. Terje's 'death' at the hands of Jon Ogdell, ex-business executive and anti-haemophile campaigner currently serving a life sentence in a high-security prison, had shocked the nation and promoted heated discussions and increased awareness around the obstacles surrounding haemophile rights. I had more human reasons for wanting to keep him to myself, but the arrangement suited us all, more or less.

But of course, for every inroad paved, the louder and more extreme the backlash.

I'd had a better Internet connection and sturdier landline installed at Glenroe out of necessity, but I didn't read the news and I wasn't on social media. I had no desire to keep track of the messy and divisive politics surrounding haemophiles' attempts to co-exist with humans. However, some news was impossible to avoid, so I was certain it wasn't a coincidence that Novák had started reaching out at a time when some powerful political names were gathering support for stricter haemophile registration laws.

I almost returned the call. Perhaps he had answers... Perhaps he could help me understand why Terje, who had stated he wanted to be with me and away from everything else, didn't seem able to stick with it for very long...

But I forced my thumb away from the call button. It wasn't in Novák's interest, or maybe even in his power, to help me understand Terje. And whatever it was that the political mogul wanted, it wouldn't be good.

I deleted his messages and opened the only one left, from a mobile number I didn't recognize.

We need to talk.
Meg

I stared at the text message long enough for Clem to stop work and ask what was up.

"Nothing," I muttered, deleting that text too and replacing the phone on the windowsill.

I returned to the Triumph and began to sand away the scratched paintwork. With the noise filling my head and the paint dust clouding around me, it was easier to ignore my thoughts. For the first time in a long time, I felt like I needed it.

The afternoon passed with surprising speed. Clem rumbled off down the track in his Land Rover around six, not having said another word. I locked the workshop as the sun began to sink behind the mountains and, finally, the air started to cool. I climbed the path to Glenroe and was relieved to find that the construction crew was gone for the day.

The ancient oak front doors had been retained, but new hinges allowed the heavy leaves to open smoothly, swinging inward with barely more than a whisper. It still felt wrong, almost intrusive, to be entering that way. When they had been in regular use, the doors had been opened by a footman—then by the housekeeper. Then, when Dad had drunk away the last servants' wages, the late Lord Aviemore had opened them himself, but only to guests he was both expecting and deemed appropriate. Those soon dwindled in number, until they'd stopped altogether as the cellars emptied, the hall decayed and the old judge retreated too far from the world to ever find his way back.

I locked them then checked that all the other doors and windows were secure. After a moment's deliberation, I fetched a shotgun from the cabinet in the cellar and returned to the caves. I stood again on the cliff over dark nothingness, holding my breath. Not even the sound of dripping water reached me.

"Is there someone here?" The words were shockingly loud in the black silence. They echoed then faded then fell away to nothing. "I know you're a haemophile." My grip tightened on the gun. Still nothing. Finally, I called, "Terje?"

Nothing.

I took a deep breath to ease my tight throat and returned to the main house, double-checking the locks on every door as I went.

I heated some leftover beef stew on the hob in the new ceramic-and-chrome kitchen and drank a bottle of Bordeaux with dinner. Having lived off microwave meals and budget tinned goods for most of my adult life, the novelty of eating and drinking well had not worn off. It had allowed me to build the muscle back that I'd lost during the lonely, hungry years at Glenroe before Terje had arrived, when both the means and inclination to eat properly had been lacking. I now filled my clothes better, had more energy and I was grateful that Terje's mysterious income extended to making sure my comforts and needs were seen to just as much, if not more so, than his own. But, as always, when alone, it wasn't the same…

I daydreamed of being with Terje, of tasting his rich, dark mouth, his pale, fresh skin — the deep, intoxicating pull of his haemophile Blood that he allowed me to indulge in when we made love.

I shook my head. It was Terje I missed, not his Blood — Terje's cool gaze and strong hands, his ready wit and earnest, intense manner. The way he looked at me like I was a complex but engaging puzzle and the slow-burning, intense passion I could coax out of him, sometimes over the course of hours.

It was all that I longed for — not the Blood.

I put a lid on the line of thought and cleared my dishes.

The ache at Terje's absence shifted around my body as I opened the door to the master bedroom. I had doubted I'd ever feel at home in a space that had been so thoroughly my father's, but, somehow, all remnants of his ghost had been removed...even if it still haunted other parts of the house in the long, dark winter nights.

The wood paneling had all been stripped away, the walls re-plastered and whitewashed. Terje had found landscape paintings by modern artists, impressionist oil works that captured the wild, ragged beauty of nature we both adored, but without the grim, neo-classical stamp of the artists who had hung in the house for generations. The black marble fireplace was clean, the iron grate removed and replaced with a state-of-the-art wood-burner. In winter it would burn for hours once lit, keeping the room warm and filling it with the cozy, comforting glow of firelight.

The heavy Victorian furniture, along with the eighteenth-century mahogany bed, was also gone. Some of it had been too decayed to restore. The bed had been salvageable, but it wasn't something I would have ever been able to sleep in, let alone do anything else. It had sold at auction for a truly staggering amount of money, and we'd used the proceeds to commission a king-sized oak four-poster, which was simple and sturdy in design, with thick blackout curtains of midnight blue.

Another set of blackout curtains framed the wide window. They allowed Terje to stay here with me until full sunrise. They also allowed me to sleep through the daylight and wake with him at sunset without as much trouble.

I got into bed, breathing deep the fresh smells of the linen where the faintest winter-crisp scent of Terje still lingered. I turned onto my side, knowing I had a long drive the next day. But thoughts of the caves and the deleted phone messages kept me awake long after I'd turned off the light.

Chapter Two

The next day dawned bright and warm, the sky azure and unblemished by clouds. I left the house just as the first construction workers arrived, keen to be on the road before McGregor or anyone else could ask any more questions.

By the time I was bowling along the A9 with the top down on the E-type Jaguar, my spirits had, if not exactly lifted, then at least steadied. The air rushing past smelled of summer heather and hot tarmac, and the beautiful machine handled so wonderfully that I couldn't help but be soothed.

I made it to the outskirts of Edinburgh in record time and enjoyed steering around the twisting, climbing streets. The city air was close, heavy with the smells of restaurants and warm stone, filled with the noise of people and traffic and the folk musicians busking on the Royal Mile. I was almost an hour early to the offices of Graeme Byrnes, but the receptionist assured me that Mr. Byrnes would be happy to see me sooner and that I could sit in the waiting area until he was free.

I took a seat and dared to check my phone. I didn't want to admit the strength of my relief when I hadn't received any more mysterious messages either from Novák or Meg, though for very different reasons. However, it didn't balance the disappointment at still finding nothing from Terje, not even a text to say he wasn't going to make the trip.

"Alec? Alec MacCarthy?"

I startled. A man about my own age stood in the doorway. He was tall and slim, dressed in gray-washed jeans and a figure-hugging polo-neck shirt, despite the warm weather, that nonetheless did little to hide the toned torso beneath. His eyes, wide with surprise, were a deep, dark brown, somewhere between black coffee and chocolate. His hair was the barest shade lighter, buzzed in a fashionable fade down the sides but long on top, falling stylishly over one eye. His lips were full and smiling, his skin the warm tone of fresh-baked bread, and he wore a single gold stud in his right ear. He was astonishingly beautiful, so much so that I felt increasingly foolish when seconds stretched by and I couldn't place him.

When a spark of amusement lit in his eyes, I finally recognized him. "Jesus. Jay?"

My old college friend's face flushed with pleasure as he came forward. "It *is* you. Bloody hell, how long has it been?"

I stood and took his offered hand in a bit of a daze. "Graduation, wasn't it? 2002?"

"Christ, so nearly twenty years. How is that possible?" He laughed, an unfettered, cheery sound that seemed to fill the air and my body all at once.

"Mad, right?" I managed. "I almost didn't recognize you."

"Well, yeah," Jay smiled a little bashfully, shrugging his leather satchel higher on his shoulder. "I lost the weight and found out it was a dairy intolerance that messed with my skin."

I hoped my own embarrassed smile looked sincere. "You look great."

Jay beamed. "Thanks. Not looking so bad yourself—but then you always did the dark and brooding thing well." He broke off with a nervous laugh. "Sorry. It's just...wow, Alec MacCarthy. It's like seeing a ghost. Oh, Jesus." His face fell. "Alec, I'm sorry."

I battled confusion for a second then my stomach dipped. "It's okay."

"No, it's not," Jay said, taking the seat next to mine. I sat and schooled my face as my old friend kept his hand on my arm while he stared earnestly into my face. "What happened to you..."

"Jay—"

"No, it needs to be said, Alec. The death of Terje Kristiansen was a tragedy and an outrage. I couldn't believe it when I heard your name on the news. Fuck, I can't even imagine..."

"It was...hard," I said carefully.

Jay pressed his lips together. For one terrible moment, I was certain he was about to cry, but he took a breath, and when he continued, his voice was level, if a little strained. "You're strong, Alec. You always were. But you shouldn't have to be."

"Maybe," I hedged, looking hopefully at the door, but there was no sign of anyone fetching me for the meeting. "What are you doing here, anyway?" I went on before he could say anything more. "I thought you lived down south?"

"I do," Jay said. "London. I'm here doing research." He opened his satchel and started rooting through it.

"Research?"

"I'm writing a book," he said, pulling out a business card.

Jason Singh, Investigative Journalist.

"What sort of book?" I asked, the sinking feeling returning.

"An investigation into human-haemo relations and what's being done about the injustices and inequalities in the UK. And what's not being done, more importantly. Graeme Byrnes provides specialist haemophile services. Did you know that?"

"I'd heard something of the sort."

"They do customized installations for communes and the ones now choosing to live independently." He looked over his shoulder and lowered his voice. "Personally, I think they just spotted a gap in the market. But it's progress, whatever the motivation — and brave, considering the flack they've had."

"Yeah, I'd heard that too."

"So what are *you* doing here?"

I hoped my hesitation wasn't obvious. "They're restoring Glenroe. They do Jacobean architecture as well."

"Finally doing the place up, huh?"

"That's right."

Jay mused a moment, eyes bright. "Say, Alec," he said, leaning closer. "How would you feel about giving me an interview?"

"Jay —" I began, shaking my head.

"It's so important, what you have to say. Your experience."

"No," I said, then, seeing his hurt expression, softened my tone. "Sorry, Jay. But I don't like talking about what happened."

Jay nodded stiffly. "Yeah. Yeah, of course not. I understand. I'm sorry for asking, but I had to chance it. You're one of the highest-profile victims of haemo-human crime. Your story could make such a difference."

"I'm sorry," I said, passing the card back.

"Keep it," Jay said, a tentative smile returning. "We should get together some time. In fact..." He stopped when the receptionist knocked on the doorframe.

"Lord Aviemore? Mr. Byrnes will see you now."

"Thank you," I said, rising. Jay stood too but stopped me leaving with a hand on my elbow.

"I'm around for the rest of the day. Want to grab lunch once you're done here?" I hesitated, but Jay added hurriedly, "I promise, no interview. It's just...it would be great to catch up." His smile was warm, his eyes clear and hopeful. It was so refreshing to be able to read someone's face, and I couldn't ignore the rush of pleasure it generated.

"Sure. That'd be great."

Jay beamed. "You've got my number. See you later."

* * * *

Duncan Byrnes reassured me that they were on schedule for finishing soon and that McGregor's concerns had been addressed.

"Thank you. I appreciate that."

"My pleasure, my lord. Oh, and just one thing before you leave…" Byrnes was a gray-haired man in his late fifties with a strong jaw and a syrupy Edinburgh accent. He also had the uncanny ability to communicate when he was about to venture into delicate territory without changing either his expression or his tone of voice. I eyed him warily until he continued. "Our mutual friend Ivor Novák has been in touch. He hopes you will make contact with him…and soon."

"Did he say why?"

Byrnes smiled a conciliatory smile. "Afraid not, my lord. But I got the impression it was a matter of some importance."

I thanked him and left, grateful to get back out into the bustle of the city and feel the sun on my face. I wandered down the Royal Mile, pulling out my phone at intervals, debating whether or not to call Novák's office. *Maybe he is with Terje – or maybe Terje is in trouble.*

My skin chilled despite the warmth of the day. I halted outside the towering facade of St. Giles Cathedral without really seeing it. I shook my head. Novák would surely say if there was a genuine emergency. No, the haemophile wanted something. And as grateful as I was for everything he'd done, all I wanted, had ever wanted, was to be left alone.

I returned my phone to my pocket and my knuckles brushed against Jay Singh's business card. I looked at it for a moment, then my stomach rumbled.

Why not?

Soon I was ducking through the low doorway of World's End pub at the bottom of the Royal Mile. Jay waved from his table in the corner. I weaved my way through the hot, packed room, which smelled strongly of beer and pub chips, remembering all the reasons I liked to be away from people. Still, I couldn't help but smile at the pleased expression on my old friend's face as I joined him. We ordered our food and Jay insisted on getting the first round of beers. I sipped the cool lager appreciatively.

"So, how've you been? You, know, since it all happened?" I leveled a look at Jay over my pint glass. "Not digging," he said, lifting his hands in a gesture of innocence, "I swear. Just asking as a friend."

I looked into my beer. "There are good days and bad days."

"Yeah, I bet. Shit, man. I really am sorry."

"It's fine. Tell me about you," I went on, not caring if the switch of subject was obvious. "I heard you got married?"

"Engaged," Jay said, looking uncomfortable. "But it didn't work out."

I cursed myself silently. "I'm sorry."

"Don't be," Jay said, smiling. "It was a good thing."

"Yeah?"

"Yeah," Jay said with a shrug. "I finally got my head around what you knew all along."

I blinked. "What's that?"

"That I'm not into women."

I raised my eyebrows, trying to decide if his expression had changed. "Wow. Well. Yeah, at uni I wasn't sure. But you always said—"

"Yeah, I know." Jay sipped his beer. "My folks always wanted the standard for me, you know—a wife, kids. It's hard to see past that stuff sometimes."

I was grateful when the food arrived to get me out of having to reply. Jay took a wolfish bite of his haggis burger with every appearance of relish, and I loaded my fork with fried fish, savoring, the sharp, vinegary tang and trying to remember the last time I'd had a meal out. Haemo-friendly hotels might be becoming more of a thing, but as they didn't eat what humans did, I doubted I'd ever be able to sit down to a meal in a romantic restaurant with Terje.

"Still," Jay said after he'd cleared his mouth with more beer, "better late than never, right?"

I smiled in response, startled by the prickling his look started at the base of my spine. "Yeah, I guess so."

"Shame I missed out on a bit of formative fun at uni, though," he went on, the look in his eyes unmistakable. "But you know what it's like when your brain says one thing and your heart — and other parts — say another."

I speared a chip. "Not really. I've always known. Guess I was lucky that way."

Jay frowned thoughtfully. "Nah, there was a girl once, wasn't there?"

"Was there?"

"Mel…or something?"

I looked at my plate. "Meg."

"Yeah, that was it. She was involved in what happened, wasn't she? And back in the day, she visited the house a few times. I remember that. She was sound. Good looking, too."

"It wasn't like that."

Jay looked at me curiously. "Are you telling me you never even tried —?"

"No," I said, raising my glass again only to realize it was empty.

Jay raised his eyebrows. "Sorry. I just always thought you might have had a bit of a thing for her."

"I dated her brother. Meg and I were just friends."

Jay's face was solemn. "Did she know that?"

I scraped the last of my mushy peas together. "She does now."

"Ah-ha," Jay said with a sympathetic look. "Yeah. Been there, mate."

I laid down my knife and fork and nodded to Jay's glass. "Another?"

Jay drained his drink then held the glass out. I was glad of the chance to head for the bar but could feel Jay's eyes on me the whole time. When I returned with the drinks, he thankfully seemed happy to change the subject.

"So you're doing up Glenroe? Finally planning to sell?"

"No," I said, forcing back my instinctive reaction to bristle whenever anyone brought up the subject of putting the hall on the market. I took a breath to allow the anger to dispel and made an attempt to think of a normal, conversational answer. "No, not selling. I came into a bit of cash, so thought it was about time to make the place habitable."

"Congratulations," Jay said, smiling again. "I remember seeing pictures of it. Quite a pile. You don't get lonely?"

My skin flushed in response to the unasked question. "I like it that way."

Jay laughed. "Of course. You always were the loner. Couldn't drag you to the pub for love nor money."

"Too many people."

Jay chuckled. "Still, on a serious note, if you ever did want to rejoin civilization, you wouldn't have any trouble selling. That place would be perfect for a haemo commune. There are caves under it, right? And it's secluded, remote…"

Jay is just chatting, I reminded myself. This was how normal people talked. Just because he'd expressed an interest didn't automatically mean there was something else going on — even if, in the past, there always had been.

"The thought had crossed my mind," I said. "But it's my home. I'm not planning to sell."

"Can't say I blame you," Jay said, his face growing serious. "I'd escape society right now if I could. Oh," he said, scowling over my shoulder at the TV hanging over the bar. "Speak of the devil and she shall appear."

I craned my neck. There was a news report on, muted but with subtitles. A large, maroon-suited woman with honey-gray hair and a forbidding expression stood at a podium, an equally large and grim-faced man stood at her shoulder. The flashes of cameras washed the scene white every few seconds and she was speaking with her head held high and her piercing gaze sweeping the reporters.

"*...and that's why we must take action now,*" the subtitles read. "*This is not a suppression of freedom, but a matter of safety. Leniency has already resulted in injury and death of innocent people...men, women and children. I acknowledge that the haemophile community aren't a wholesale threat, but their very nature means risk is high, whatever their conscious intentions. There must be more measures, like with any potentially dangerous animal, to ensure the public's safety. The licensing of independent haemophile habitations must stop and stricter security imposed on existing communes — *"

"Absolutely unbelievable," Jay muttered.

"Who is she?"

"Allegra Brassington. And that charming fella behind her is her husband, Edgar. You've seriously never heard of the Brassingtons?"

"I know the name."

"Officious, right-wing bigots, the pair of them," Jay said, anger transforming his face. "The damage they're doing is unbelievable. They shouldn't be allowed—"

"Jay," I started, shifting in my seat.

"It's important," Jay insisted. "They're promoting hatred and bigotry."

"They're politicians. What else is new?"

Jay regarded me for a long, startled moment, something between anger and pain darkening his eyes. "You seriously have no interest in any of this? After everything you went through?"

I glared. "What happened to me wasn't about any cause or a campaign. People like that"—I gestured at the couple on the screen—"*and* people like you just use these things for your ends. The only difference between them and you is that they *know* they're doing it for themselves. But none of you, *none* of you, know what really happened. None of you understand. Don't pretend you do."

Jay stared, his dark eyes wide. Eventually, he blinked and looked away. "I...I'm sorry," he said softly. I drank my beer, already regretting the ferocity of the outburst, if not the content of it. Jay leaned over the table and put his hand on mine. The touch sent sparks up my arm. "I'm sorry I upset you. And I'm sorry I gave you the impression that any of this is about me. It isn't, Alec. I swear. My editor wanted me to steer well clear of the whole thing. She thinks it's a career-killer. But I can't, Alec." He squeezed my hand and I attempted to control the effect it had on me. "I can't let it alone. Haemophiles need human champions." His tone softened further, as did the look in his eyes. "You know that better than most."

I pulled my hand away. The noise and heat and smell of the pub pressed in on me. I suddenly longed for Terje with a deep, keen passion and was more aware than ever of how far apart we were.

Jay startled me back to reality by laying a hand on my cheek. His warm, beer-scented breath brushed my lips. His eyes were burning. I took a gentle hold of his hand and removed it from my face.

"I'm sorry."

Jay was quiet, but then his disappointment melted behind another soft smile. "It's okay, Alec. I understand." He leaned forward and pressed a soft, chaste kiss to my cheek. I was momentarily surrounded by the smell of woody aftershave undercut by the musky, natural scene of a human male. But then Jay was standing, pulling out his wallet and waving away my protests. "I insist. Besides, I can put it on expenses." His smile remained, even if the sadness hadn't left his eyes. "Good luck, Alec," he said, shouldering his bag. "Stay in touch, okay? And look me up if you're ever in London."

Jay went to the bar, paid the bill and left, pausing at the door to raise a hand in farewell. I stared at his empty seat and half-drank beer for a long time, trying to figure out what had happened. Not Jay's part of it… I understood that well enough. But I didn't understand my own, my reaction and the undeniable comfort I had got from looking across the table and understanding just what was going through the other person's mind.

I finished my own beer, then Jay's, then ordered another.

By the time the sun was setting and I was heading to the hotel, I was more than a little drunk, but it had done little to improve my mood. The bartender hadn't helped by giving me that half-sympathetic, half-wary look people wore when they finally realized where they knew me from. That was the moment I had decided to continue my descent into oblivion in private.

I let myself into the luxurious room with a sigh. The air-conditioned space was pleasantly cool, but I went straight to the balcony windows and opened them wide, keen to let in the summer night, the sounds of the bustling city and the smell of exhaust and heated tarmac—anything to distract me from who wasn't there. I emptied the fridge of its miniature bottles of whiskey, rum and vodka and dumped them on the bed. I leaned into the soft pillows, giving the door to the lightproof sleeping cell next to the bathroom a glare as I twisted the cap off the whiskey.

I emptied it into my mouth in one, enjoying the warmth it spread down my throat. I opened the vodka next and took a sip, grimacing at the taste, then emptied that too. I threw the bottle on the floor and stared at the ceiling. The bed was very soft and smelled of laundered linen and lavender. I ran my fingers over the soft fabric, thinking what a waste it was to be here alone.

I began kneading my cock through my jeans but felt nothing other than a faint stir beneath the numbing swirl of alcohol. I sighed and dropped my hand. I bit my lip, then closed my eyes and visualized Jay's suggestive smile, remembering the smell of human skin and clean hair.

The blood started to pool in my groin, but then the bed dipped. I started and sat up. Terje sat on the end of the bed, his pale, blue-white hair tucked behind his ears, his silver eyes glinting in the low light. He was so beautiful that I was convinced he must be a dream. But then he laid his long-fingered hand on my shin. The pressure was real.

"Hello, Alec."

I blinked, the dozens of things I'd wanted to say to him tumbling out of my head.

"You didn't think I was coming, did you?"

I swallowed, still reluctant to move, worried the spell would break and Terje would vanish. "Where have you been?"

"That's not important."

Anger came rushing back. "A month, Terje. You've been gone a month — no word, no nothing."

Instead of answering, Terje shrugged off his jacket and pulled his black T-shirt over his head. My breath caught in my throat, as it always did when I took in the smooth, toned lines of the unblemished torso, the lean, muscled arms, the skin of an unearthly color between fresh snow and warm milk. From his paleness, I knew he needed to feed and I felt an answering spark of excitement, knowing how intense sex could be when he was hungry.

I tried to speak again, the hurt and the questions still sticking like claws in my chest, but Terje climbed on top of me and captured my mouth. My control, along with any remaining thoughts of Jay, evaporated like mist under the rays of the morning sun. He kissed me deeply, tasting the inside of my mouth and swallowing, breathing deep as he did so, like he was consuming every aspect of me. As I ran my hands up his back, the familiar shape and feel of the iron-hard muscles sliding under the silk-smooth skin allowed my arousal to fight through the alcohol. I was painfully hard in seconds.

Terje made a low noise, and I knew he'd felt it. Knowing my desire stoked his sent another stab of pleasure down my spine. I sat up enough to unbutton and throw away my shirt while Terje undid my jeans. I rid myself of them and my underwear, then fumbled impatiently at the button on Terje's pants. He removed them, then I lay back, pulling Terje on top, comforted and exhilarated as I always was by the surprising weight of his slight, lean frame. I buried my face in his neck, mouthing the sensitive skin just under his ear and breathing in his startling fresh, clean smell. No musk there. No scent of sweat or shampoo or aftershave. He was, as always, the cool but heady smell of wind over the autumn moors, heavy with fading sunshine and sharp with incoming snow.

"Alec," he breathed in my ear. I quivered to hear my name in his accented voice, already tight with need. I kissed him again, delving my tongue deep into his mouth. I brushed his sharp canines with my tongue and groaned, not realizing until that moment just how much I'd missed his wonder and the strangeness. Sensing my urgency, Terje sat up. I rose too, keeping our bodies pressed together, thrusting just to feel friction against my straining erection. I fumbled a hand between us and grasped Terje's cock. It was only half-hard, but Terje gasped into my mouth. I forced myself to slow, knowing that if I kept this pace, I'd be done before Terje had even gotten started.

The kiss went on and his grip began to tighten on my shoulders. Finally, Terje was hard in my hand and he broke the kiss to fling his head back and arch into my hold. I licked at his collarbone and shoulder.

"Alec," he breathed again, wrapping his hand around mine to still my ministrations. His cheeks were flushed, his lips swollen with kissing, the dark black of his pupils expanded so that only the tiniest thread of silver iris remained. As I watched, he pricked his index finger against his canine. A red-black drop of Blood swelled on the pad. He held it to my mouth and the thick smell of strong wine and autumn fruit flooded my senses. My entire body thrummed with anticipation, but I held back, as I always did, just so I knew I could, then I took the finger into my mouth.

The taste and smell filled me like hot water welling up from a thermal spring. My own blood rushed into every inch of my frame and thumped in my rigid cock. I closed my eyes, fighting the terrifying second that always came where I felt I might be lost forever. But then my heartbeat slowed to a thick, strong slug, my skin began to tingle and I was aware of every fiber of the covers under me, every curve and contour of Terje's body and the slow, warm sound of our hearts beating in time.

I opened my eyes to gaze into the molten fire of Terje's eyes. When we kissed again and I knew I was feeling, tasting and smelling everything he was, the heat of my desire flared to a raging furnace.

This feeling of being together on a Blood-high, naked and kissing, would almost have been enough on its own. But as Terje's need grew more desperate, his kiss became harsher, his teeth catching my lip. I tasted hot cooper. Terje swallowed at it hungrily then started to lick and kiss where my shoulder met my neck.

"Now, Alec. Please."

I took a deep breath and slid my hand around Terje's toned, smooth hip and over the curve of his arse. Slowly, I pressed two fingers into him. He went rigid then let out a long, low sound, closer to a cry than a groan, and I had to take a moment to marshal my own reactions. Even with the tempering effect of the Blood, I was still human, and it was still possible to come too soon.

I pushed my fingers farther in, reaching the place that made him curse in Norwegian. I added another and rubbed them over the spot again and again. Only when he was panting and begging into my hair did I withdraw my fingers. Terje lifted himself, then slowly lowered onto my cock. He glided down in one smooth motion, tightening his hands on my shoulders to the point of pain. My flesh shivered and sang as the tight, warm heat enveloped me. I let out a low groan, enraptured by knowing that, finally, we were together again.

Terje moved slowly at first, his eyes shut, holding so tight that his fingernails pierced my skin, the sharp counterpoints of pain deliciously punctuating the deep, slow heat radiating out from my crotch. I held still and let Terje take his pleasure, watching hypnotized as his face transformed. The steel-strong control that usually masked his expression melted away and he became pleasure-hungry and helpless—his mouth open, eyes shut, his forehead pressed against mine, panting hot, wet breath against my face as he rode me.

Terje had tried to describe how fucking made him feel. He said it was like the only thing that mattered in the world was the sensation of me in him—the way it completely changed the way he was able to think and feel and yearn.

It made him feel human again.

Just watching him was like nothing I had ever known before with any other partner or in the deepest and most personal possibilities of my own imaginings.

And I knew that even if I lived forever, I would never be able to get enough of it.

Terje increased his pace, his breathing coming in hitched gasps. He opened his eyes and stared deep into mine as the thunderstorm of impending orgasm started to gather under my belly. I shifted, adjusted my angle and Terje cried my name. I reached between us and grasped his now-weeping cock.

Three firm pulls and Terje was coming, hot and hard, in my hand. He made a high-pitched, helpless noise. The hard muscles clamped around me and the world vanished in an explosion of heat, fire and hurricane, blinding and deafening me to everything except the tidal wave of ecstasy.

Chapter Three

"You're tired."

Terje was brushing his long fingers through the hair on my chest. I forced my eyes open, fighting back the warm oblivion that had threatened to steal me away.

"No, I'm not."

Terje chuckled softly and extricated himself from my arms. I made a noise of protest, propping myself on my elbows as Terje started to collect his clothing from the floor.

"What are you doing?"

"You should sleep," Terje said, pulling on his jeans.

"This is the first night we've had together in weeks," I muttered, taking Terje by the wrist and pulling him close. "I'm not going to sleep for any of it."

Terje brushed a kiss across my forehead. "If you're sure..."

"Of course I'm sure," I said, annoyance bleeding into my tone.

Terje, either not noticing or not caring about my reaction, continued to dress, pulling on his T-shirt, shoes and light, black jacket. He always wore muted tones, blacks and grays, sometimes pale blues. It should make someone with his pale complexion look washed-out or even sickly. But against his smooth, pearlescent skin and hair, it just made him look exotic, unearthly, surreal but achingly beautiful.

"Are we going somewhere?" I asked, breaking off from staring to retrieve my underwear.

"I'd like to go for a walk," Terje said, pulling a band out of his pocket and tying his blue-white hair back into a tail. As I was the only one available to cut it and I wasn't the best hairdresser, he'd allowed it to grow long again. The shorter strands at the front fell into his eyes, but it left the smooth lines of his neck free.

"Where?"

"In the park," he replied, fetching a bottle from a bag he'd dropped in the corner. "Below the castle."

"They have that here," Alec said, indicating the fridge.

"I prefer my own," he replied. He opened the bottle, drank deeply and color washed into his cheeks. He dropped the empty bottle in the specialist canister next to the fridge and went toward the window.

"This is a safe place," I muttered, grabbing a fresh shirt out of my case. "You don't have to go out of the window."

"It's better to be careful," he said, then was gone.

I sighed, trying to fight the return of my frustration. I finished dressing and hurried out into the busy city night. The air had cooled but the towering stone buildings still retained some of the warmth from the day, giving the air an enclosed feel. The sky arched black overhead, bleached featureless by streetlight.

Terje was nowhere in sight. I crossed the North Bridge, heading for Market Street and the way down into the Princes Street Gardens. The noise of people weaving between the bars, clubs and restaurants fell away as I descended the stairs into the cool, fresh openness of the park. A train heading into Waverley station hissed by on the rails above. As I ventured farther in to where the only light was from the LED lampposts installed to lower light pollution, the stars finally became visible, glittering like diamonds on a sheet of black velvet.

Edinburgh Castle glowered from its clifftop, all ramparts, towers and impossibly large blocks of stone. I had always thought it looked forbidding, but when Terje stepped out of the shadows to stand at my side and gaze up at it in quiet wonder, I tried again to see it how he might see it.

"*It's beautiful, in its own way,*" he had said the first time we had visited Edinburgh, almost a year before. "*It's a promise to protect as well as to fight back.*"

Looking at his profile in the starlight, my anger faded, and for the moment, I was just grateful he was back.

He laced his long fingers through my own. The memory of Jay touching that same hand earlier that day rose in my mind but I shook it away, along with the ghosting guilt. Terje sent me a sideways look and I was suddenly certain, however impossible it was, that he knew. But then he started to walk down the path, drawing me with him.

"We have a story about a haemophile that lived in the castle in the Middle Ages," Terje murmured as we walked. "Did I tell you that?"

"No, you didn't. I've heard lots of ghost stories about it," I said absently. "Never anything about vampires."

"It's one of *our* stories. Like a cautionary folk tale…"

"Cautionary?"

Terje's forehead creased slightly in the pale light. "Very few of our kind have ever lived outside of a commune. This one did. Her story, well...it doesn't end well."

"Is it true?"

"I'm sure parts of it are. But I've heard it told in lots of different ways over the years. They all talk of her living in the dungeons, though—some say for a year, some say a century—feeding on prisoners and guards."

"What happened to her?" I asked, though I was sure I could guess.

"She was killed. Burned at the stake. The humans thought she was a witch. People were very inventive with their cruelty in those days."

"I'd say they still are."

Terje gave me an unreadable look.

"So this story," I asked, cautiously. "It was a warning? About haemophiles trying to live on their own?"

Terje's silver eyes were dark in the moonlight. I was suddenly desperate with the need to know what lay behind them, but I kept my mouth shut, hoping, praying Terje would volunteer something personal without me having to push. My chest clenched when he opened his mouth to reply, but then his gaze slid over my shoulder and sharpened. I looked around. An older couple with an Aberdeen terrier were ambling along the path, wrapped in coats despite the warm summer night. I turned back and Terje was gone.

I hid my surprise and ensuing frustration with an effort. I stepped off the path as the couple wandered past, pretending to admire the castle. They nodded and smiled a little warily. I returned the smile as best I could, then fidgeted until they were out of sight.

I scanned the shadowy paths and trees, then Terje stepped out of nowhere, his hands in his pockets, like he'd been waiting there the whole time.

"Was that really necessary?"

"I can't be seen, Alec," Terje said. "You know this."

"Things are different now," I argued. "You don't have to hide."

"Others of my kind don't, no," Terje replied in that soft, reasonable tone he always used when I was being unreasonable. "*I* do."

"Do you really think they would have recognized you?"

"They recognized *you*." I scuffed the path with my foot, remembering the look in their eyes. "I'm sorry this is difficult, Alec. But we knew it was never going to be easy."

"Where were you, Terje?" I hadn't meant to ask. Asking threatened the delicate bubble that existed around the things we never discussed. That bubble protected what we could share. But it had never stopped chafing that it existed at all.

"Why do you want to know?"

"Because I don't like not knowing where you are for weeks at a time," I started, and found, now that I'd started, I couldn't stop. "That's something I would never have to explain to anyone else."

"Anyone human."

I made an impatient noise. "We've been together nearly two years, Terje. Don't you trust me?"

"It's not a matter of trust, Alec. It's a matter of protection."

"Whose? Yours or mine?"

"Both of us."

I took a moment to gather my patience. "Do you see Novák on these little jaunts of yours?"

"Sometimes."

"Do you see any other haemophiles?"

"No." Terje actually looked annoyed. "That would be foolish, even if I wanted to. Why does that matter?"

I let out a shuddering breath. "We agreed to make a life together, away from everything. But I guess I'm worried now that it's not enough for you."

Terje gazed into my face. "You're missing your own kind, so you're worried I am too."

"No, that's not —"

"You are all I need, Alec."

"Then tell me where you go."

He began walking again, choosing a path that would take us deeper into the park. I fell into step beside him, resisting the urge to prompt. Eventually, he let out a quiet sigh.

"Most of the time, I'm just out walking."

"Where?"

"Anywhere. Everywhere. The Highlands, the National Parks, the coast. I just like to see new places…to spend time alone. I thought you understood that."

My chest clenched. "And the rest of the time?"

"The rest of the time?"

"You said *most of the time*. What about the rest?"

He drew in a breath, not meeting my eyes. "Recently I've been standing watch…for Novák."

"Standing watch for *what*?"

He was silent for such a long time that I thought he wasn't going to answer. But then, finally, "Evgeniya."

I stopped walking. "Your Magister? She's back?"

"It appears so."

"Where?"

"We don't know…not exactly."

"Can't she sense you when you're near?"

"I'm careful."

I ran a hand through my hair, skin crawling on my arms and back. "Novák should be working with the police, Interpol…not you."

"He did try. But they can't hold her, even if they find her."

"Things are never going to change if haemophiles keep fighting these battles on their own."

"That is why I didn't want to tell you," Terje said, recommencing walking. "Now you're scared."

"I'm not scared." Terje gave me a look. "Okay, I'm a reasonable amount of scared," I countered. "Why aren't you? If she knows you're alive, the truth coming out will be the least of our worries."

"You asked me to trust you, Alec, so I've told you the truth. I've told you I'm careful. That should be enough."

"I just don't understand why you want to be involved," I said defeatedly.

"I owe Novák, Alec. We both do."

"I know, but this—"

"We may be separate from the world and I'm happy with that, whatever you might think. But I still care about what happens to my people…and yours. Don't you?"

I stared into the trees. "Not really."

"You don't mean that."

"Don't I?"

"When you thought Megan Carlisle was in danger, you did everything you could to protect her."

I shoved my hands in my pockets and didn't meet his eye. "She's Meg Daile now. She got married, remember?"

Terje frowned. "Stop trying to change the subject. Evgeniya is a threat to everyone, Alec, not just me. I'm just doing my bit."

"How, exactly?"

"Watching. Listening. I can't explain all of it."

"Just promise me you're not putting yourself at risk."

"I'm protecting us, Alec—and what we have. That's worth any amount of risk."

We turned a corner, and the castle came into view again. The stars were remote, cold pinpricks over its crenelations. I didn't answer. I knew he was right. But his being right didn't make it any easier to accept.

"You yearn for your own kind too...sometimes. I know you do."

I stopped walking. "What do you mean?"

"I can smell him on you."

Heat flooded my face, even as my hands and feet went cold. "It's not what you think."

"It's okay," Terje said, laying a hand on my arm. "I understand. I promise."

I stopped walking. "Understand *what*?"

"That maybe I can't give you everything you need," he continued calmly. "I wouldn't be angry, you know—if you decided to you wanted...time...with another human."

I took a moment to make sure my voice would be steady. "You're telling me you don't care if I sleep around?"

"I don't think I know what that phrase means. But if you mean would I be angry if you had sex with another human? No, I wouldn't."

"Does that mean *you're* sleeping round?" My voice was harsh in the still night air.

"Why would you assume that?"

"You just told me fucking our own kind isn't a big deal."

"You misunderstand."

"I don't think I do. McGregor's men..." I tried to hold my emotion in check, but it burned through my fingers like molten metal. "They heard something in the caves. It can't be human. Who is it, Terje?"

Terje's face was like marble. "I don't know what you're talking about."

"Don't you?"

"No, I don't. And you miss the point."

"What *is* the point?"

"Just that we're different, Alec. No amount of time together or desire to understand will change that. I've accepted it. I thought you had too."

"I know we're different," I forced out, "from each other, sure—but also from everyone else. And that's why what we have works so well. I also know that you're doing all this"—I gestured to the space between us—"to keep yourself apart from me."

A faint line appeared between his fine eyebrows. "Nothing either of us do can stop there being distance between us."

"Bullshit. You're doing it on purpose. You're scared. That's what it is. Scared of what this might become if you let it."

"You're mistaken."

"Maybe you've never had a relationship like this before. I understand if you're uncertain sometimes. So am I. But disappearing for weeks? Telling me to fuck other men?"

"That's not what I—"

"You're scared of committing to me. Why?" Terje's face was dangerously still. A very real fear threatened to damp the heat surging in my belly but wasn't enough to extinguish it.

"I'm sorry you think that," Terje said with such an air of finality that I had to fight not gather him into my arms and sob apologies into his neck. But I knew if I did that, I'd be doing it forever...and I couldn't carry on pretending.

"I want to love you, Terje."

"No, you don't. You want *me* to love *you*. That's different."

A spear of ice plunged through my chest. Terje looked up at the castle again, his mouth set in hard lines. "I have to go away again soon, Alec," he said softly. "Do we really want to spend what little time we have like this?"

I unstuck my tongue. "You're leaving again?"

Terje nodded. "I'm sorry, particularly after this." He started walking again, not meeting my eye. "But I have to."

I hurried to catch him up. "When?"

"Tomorrow night."

I grabbed his wrist to stop him moving and turned him to face me. "Where are you going?"

"That's not—"

"Where are you *going*, Terje?"

"London...to see Novák."

I sat on a bench and stared at my hands. Terje sat next to me. After a long moment he put a hand on my shoulder. I closed my eyes, trying to get on top of everything that threatened to spill out. When I finally felt like I wasn't about to burst, I opened my eyes.

"Let me come with you."

"I don't think that's a good idea."

"Novák's been trying to get hold of me."

"He has?"

"You didn't know?"

"No."

I spent a fruitless moment trying to figure out what he was thinking. "I should come."

"I thought you didn't want to be involved?"

"If it's the only way to be with you, I will."

Terje examined me in silence, then leaned forward and kissed me. I opened my mouth to his searching tongue. He delved it in deep, inhaling, swallowing my taste and smell. I opened to it and didn't push back, sensing Terje's need to just feel me. When he eventually broke away, I was already regretting everything I'd said. I had him. Even if it wasn't always, even if it wasn't forever, why did I have to push?

"I'm sorry you're upset...and I'm sorry I don't understand why."

I couldn't think of an answer and wasn't sure if one were necessary. I squeezed his hand.

"We'll go together," he said. "I'd like to know what Novák wants from you."

I managed a mischievous smile. "Jealous?"

Terje lifted one eyebrow. "Is that a real question or just something else you think I should feel?"

I sighed. "It was a joke...this time."

Terje looked down at our joined hands. "This business with Evgeniya is serious, Alec. I can't avoid being drawn in, but you can."

I thought I should be angry again, but being so close, with the clear, still night around us, I suddenly found I didn't want to be angry anymore. The knot in my stomach hadn't loosened, but for the moment at least, I resolved to pretend it wasn't there.

"There's only a couple of hours left before dawn," I said quietly, leaning in and brushing my lips under

Terje's ear, making him shiver. "Let's not talk about it anymore."

Terje smiled against my cheek and he ran his free hand up my thigh. "I would like that."

* * * *

When I woke several hours later, blinking blearily at my phone and seeing that it had yet to reach noon, I cursed himself for slipping back into a daytime cycle. I tossed and turned for another half-hour, aware that I would likely be up most of the following night, but sleep eluded me. I sighed and pushed back the covers.

The room was as dark as midnight with the blackout blinds drawn, but I didn't turn on the light, instead using my phone torch to dress. Terje was safely behind the locked door of the sleeping cell, but I moved silently out of habit, the memory and scars from the single time I'd woken him in the day both feeling fresh as when they'd been made.

I shook my head to rid myself of the image of Terje's face, transformed by the Blood sensing a threat, his lips drawn back from long, sharp teeth, eyes blazing, razor-tipped hands reaching. But the memory didn't leave me until after I'd stepped into the sunlit corridor. I took a moment to let the sunshine warm me, then, stomach growling, left the hotel.

I took a table at a chain restaurant on Princes Street, ordering three courses. I was always ravenous after a night with Terje. The fresh hairline scratches across my back pulled as I reached to pour myself a drink from the jug of water, and I smiled at the sweet, intimate sting.

I inhaled the food but turned away the wine list, thinking of the long drive to London. As I lingered over dessert, staring out at the traffic, my thoughts turned away from the previous night to the one ahead.

The news that Evgeniya was back had sent the flesh crawling over my bones. I'd seen what Terje's old Magister was capable of firsthand and had read about the other atrocities she'd committed during Blood Winter in morbid detail over the weeks that had followed. I'd also spent months thinking, like the rest of the world still did, that Terje had been killed in revenge for her actions.

The thought that she was somewhere in the UK, evading both human and haemophile law enforcement, made my blood run cold.

I paid the bill and left to spend the afternoon exploring more of the Old Town, though I gave the World's End a wide berth. I knew Jay must be safely on his way back to London, but I was still unwilling to confront the memory of what we'd shared the day before and equally unwilling to confront the reasons why.

I was back in the hotel well before sunset, packed and ready to go when Terje emerged from the sleeping cell. The soft warmth in the back of his eyes and the kiss he greeted me with helped me pretend to forget the confrontation from the day before.

The drive to London was close to seven hours, even though the sunset start meant we had clear roads most of the way. I relented somewhere in the middle of Yorkshire and pulled into a motorway service station to allow Terje to take over for the rest of the drive. Even with the Jaguar's top down and the night air blowing in our faces, I still found myself nodding off as it crept toward three a.m.

"Sleep if you want," Terje said as he changed lanes to overtake another haulage lorry, the only other traffic on the road.

"No, I'll shake it. I always do."

"A daytime cycle is more natural for you."

I refrained from arguing, yet again, that I *wanted* to be awake when he was, trying to ignore the pain that rose from him seemingly being unable to understand why.

We hit the outskirts of London just after four. Dawn was starting to pale the western sky. It was already warm, the temperature having risen the farther south we'd traveled. As the gray light brightened to yellow, I took off my jacket, sweat already gathering between my shoulder blades.

"Will we get inside in time?" I asked, taking in the sky and the white-knuckled grip Terje had on the wheel.

"Yes," he replied, his voice harsh. "We'll have to, don't we?" The ghost of a smile on his tight face did little to ease my concern.

"I still think this is a bad idea," I said, staring around at the traffic and the pedestrians already crowding the pavements. "Surely there's more risk of you being recognized here? Your commune was near London, right?"

Terje stopped at red light and pressed the button for the roof. The soft top hummed as it closed over our heads, casting us into shadow. Terje visibly eased.

"I can stay hidden when I need to," he replied. "Sorry, Alec. I need quiet. I'm concentrating."

His relief was visible when we finally turned off the main road into the concealed entrance of a subterranean parking garage under a towering building, the top of which was so high that the windows were already flashing in the fiery sunrise. The iron shutter rumbled shut behind us and Terje pulled into a space among an array of vehicles, from sports cars to four-by-four off-road trucks.

"This is Novák's building," Terje said in a tight voice as he climbed out the car and limped toward a lift. "I can sleep here. I…I don't know what you…"

"Don't worry about me," I said, knowing better than to touch him, even though I ached to do so. "Can I do anything?"

Terje shook his head. He pressed a button next to a camera set in the frame of the lift. Seconds ticked by. He leaned heavily on the wall, breathing deep, his hands clenched into fists, then, finally, the lift doors sighed open and Terje staggered inside. He waved me away when I tried to follow.

"Stay back," he rasped. "The Blood is taking over. Wait…then push the button…"

The lift doors slid shut and I was alone in the dim, silent garage. I waited a few moments to make sure the lift was on its way, then pushed the call button. For a long time nothing happened, then I was startled by the video screen flickering to life. A thin-faced middle-aged woman appeared, giving me a blank look.

"Uh, hello?" I said, bending to look into the camera. "I'm sorry. I got left down here. I'm with—"

"I know who you are," she said, her voice flat. "The lift will return for you shortly, my lord."

The screen went blank. It was almost ten minutes before the doors slid open again. I stepped in, looking around, but there were no buttons. The doors shut automatically, then I was moving up.

It seemed to take a very long time, but, finally, the doors opened again. I stepped into a wide, bright lobby. Tall windows on my left provided a spectacular view of the jagged London skyline. The sunrise made the city look like it was on fire. The woman was waiting with her hands pressed together, watching me from behind the narrow lenses of her glasses. She wore a business suit in a shade of dried-heather brown which, combined with her straw-colored hair, made me think of the lowlands under the summer sun. The look in her eyes was anything but warm, though.

"Lord Aviemore," she said. Her voice, devoid of accent, was clipped and without emotion. "A phone call would have sufficed."

I scanned the series of closed doors behind her. Everything was eerily silent. Even my feet didn't seem to make a sound as I walked to her across the deep, earth-colored carpet.

"And you are?"

"Miriam Collinson. I am Rådgiver Novák's private secretary."

"Rådgiver?"

"A Norwegian word. Roughly translates as 'professor'. He is currently in repose. I'm afraid any audience you were hoping for will have to wait until tonight."

"Do you know what he wants with me?"

"I believe it's best if the Rådgiver discusses that with you himself. Now, please, Lord Aviemore," she said, turning to one of the doors. "I'm sure your tired after your long journey. Let me escort you to somewhere you can rest."

"It's okay. I can find a hotel…"

My tone earned a sharp look over her shoulder. "I'm sure the Rådgiver would prefer you weren't spotted in London until he's had a chance to speak to you."

She led the way down a long corridor with more closed doors. She stopped at one that looked identical to all the others and opened it. I stepped into a bedroom suite with plush furnishings and more wide windows. The Thames snaked its way through the jungle of metal and glass, glowing like lava in the summer dawn.

"Please make yourself comfortable, my lord," Collinson said from the door. "Meals will be provided. Please do not attempt to leave. Someone will come for you at sunset."

She shut the door behind her. I tried the handle. It was locked. I clamped down on the unease blooming in my insides then rubbed my eyes, finally allowing myself to acknowledge how tired I was. I found the command to lower the electric blinds, casting the room into near-complete darkness, stripped and crawled between the cool, crisp sheets. I stretched an arm over the space next to me, wondering again if I'd ever get used to the idea of having a lover I would never sleep with, but my exhaustion quickly stole the thought, then my awareness, away.

Chapter Four

I woke several hours before sunset, showered in the well-appointed bathroom and ate a rather good meal of steak and potatoes that had appeared on the side table while I was washing. Finally, the sun sank below the horizon, staining the sky like spilled wine, and there was a knock at the door.

Collinson stood outside. I followed her through more anonymous, silent corridors.

"What is all this?"

"Guest accommodations," she replied while tapping a code into a keypad beside another lift.

"They're...extensive."

"There was a time when Rådgiver Novák entertained many human guests—conferences and meetings as well as social occasions. Sadly, they are largely unneeded in these present times."

The doors opened onto a wide, open-plan space, softly lit by many shaded lamps. The floor was black marble, broken here and there by deep, thick rugs in cool creams and browns. Windows on all sides looked out over the city. Thousands of lighted windows broke up the night until there was almost no darkness left. An artificial fireplace, unlit, stood in the middle, surrounded by wide, deep couches. A huge television was mounted on the wall, tuned to a news channel. The report was on the Brassingtons' recent press conference. Standing in front of the television, with his back to me, was the huge, broad-shouldered form of Ivor Novák. His black hair, falling almost to his waist, was secured in a neat tail. He wore a navy suit, tailored perfectly to his massive frame, and a crisp white shirt that set off the glow of his dark skin.

He muted the TV as we approached. Collinson announced me and withdrew. Novák finally turned to face me.

"Lord Aviemore, this is a pleasant surprise."

"Where's Terje?"

"He has not yet risen," he said, his deep voice curving slightly around a long-faded European accent. He moved to a side table and pulled the stopper from a decanter. "You arrived rather late. But I'm sure he won't be long. In the meantime, I'm grateful for the opportunity to talk to you alone. Whiskey, my lord?"

"Stop calling me that," I said, irritated.

"I'm sorry it makes you uncomfortable," he said. "Resisting your identity never ends well, you know. But as you wish. Mr. MacCarthy, please." He held out the tumbler of amber liquid. I took it and sipped. It was a single malt, peaty, probably from Islay. I took a deep swallow, willing it to still my nerves.

"Why are we here, Novák?"

"I was going to ask you the same question."

"Terje said you *summoned* him."

"That's correct."

"He says he's been working for you."

"Also correct."

"*Watching* for Evgeniya?"

Novák poured a drink for himself and swirled the whiskey around in the glass. "Among other things…yes."

"You promised us," I said. "You promised that we would be left alone."

Novák watched me over the rim of his glass as he sipped. His angled face was as readable as a cliff face. Eventually, he lowered his glass.

"I'm still hoping that one day, that will be possible. But times are…complicated. Terje agreed to help. And we need all the help we can get," he said, with a significant look at the television.

"This is not our fight."

"It's everyone's fight."

I fought impatience. "He's trying to break *away* from all this. You're keeping him tied to a life that made him miserable."

Novák poured me a second drink then filled his own glass from a bottle retrieved from a chrome refrigerator unit under the sideboard. The thick, red liquid clung to the glass like syrup. He sipped appreciatively and I tasted something bitter on my tongue.

"Terje can never break away entirely," he said softly. "I spend my nights fighting for our right to live independently, for those that want it that way. But we can't exist entirely alone. It's instinct. And it gets stronger in times of danger."

"And sending Terje to hunt his psychotic ex-Magister is keeping him out of danger?"

"I have no choice. Our security is being threatened on many fronts. From without" — he nodded at the

muted footage of the Brassingtons on the TV screen—
"and from within. There are plenty of our own kind as
opposed to change as humans, plenty who think we
should have stayed in hiding instead of finding ways
to live without killing." He lifted his glass and drank
deeply. "Evgeniya Morak is one such individual. And
she has the capacity to do more damage than any
human politician could ever hope to."

"Why would she want to?"

"The bigger the divide between our kinds, the more
support will be gained for the idea that we go back to
the way things were."

"Things can't go back—not now that we know you
exist."

"We are at good at hiding. It wouldn't be easy, and
without the institutionalized donations, it would mean
killing again, but there are plenty of our kind, I'm
ashamed to say, who would welcome that. Terje can
help stop all this before it goes too far."

"How?"

"He is able to track Evgeniya and do it discreetly."

"Because he's supposed to be dead, you mean?"

"Precisely. But that has its own drawbacks, which is
the reason I wanted to speak to you." He gestured to
the sofas. I sat stiffly on the edge. Novák folded his long
form into an armchair, drained his glass and set it aside.

"This is something I've been considering for some
time. You, Lord Aviemore, are well known among the
haemophile population. You would be able to visit and
question members of the community that Terje can't."

"Like who?"

"Like those at Forest Hill."

I frowned. "Terje's old commune?" My skin
prickled. "Why would I do that?"

"To see if they've heard from Evgeniya — and find out how they feel about her return."

I tried to think of the first question to ask. "Surely if they knew where she was, they would have told you?"

"Unlikely."

"Why?"

"Many of them will still be loyal to her."

"They would still be on her side after everything that happened?"

"There will be division" — Novák gazed out the window — "and conflict, of course. But a haemophile's first loyalty is always to their Magister. Disgraced she may be, but how the members of the commune will feel about that will be as mixed as they are. But either way, you have more of a chance of finding something out than I would."

"Why would they talk to me?"

"Because you mean something to Terje — and Terje meant something to them."

I shook my head. "They wouldn't talk to me."

"Alec's right."

I sat up. Terje was stood behind my sofa. The soft light threaded gold through his hair and eyelashes, burnishing his pale eyes to amber. "He should not be involved."

Novák rose, putting his hands in his pockets. "You've done all you can on this front, Terje. You've established she's in the country. But the fact that she's been quiet for so long has me concerned. She's planning something. We need to find out what."

"*I* will find out what."

"No," Novák shook his head. "I need you for a different task now."

"No more tasks," I stood, glaring at both of them. "No more missions. We're trying to build a life together—a life you," I said, jabbing my finger at Novák, "promised we'd have in exchange for our cooperation. This shit never ends"—I made an impatient gesture at the TV—"but it's not our problem."

Terje sighed. "It *is* our problem, Alec. How do you expect us to live in peace with Evgeniya out there planning to kill us?"

I swallowed. "You think that's why she's here?"

"Why else?"

"She doesn't even know you're alive," I protested then, with a stab of worry, "does she?"

Novák looked at me. "We don't know."

"You don't *know*? And you've got him tailing her?" I exploded. "Sending him right into her path?"

"I told you that I'm careful," Terje said.

"This woman followed us from Glasgow into the mountains without pausing to think because she could track your Blood," I said. "How can you possibly do this safely?"

"I...take something," Terje said. Novák gave him a look, but he kept his eyes on me. "Something in my feed. It helps mask me from her."

I stared. "So now you're drugging him too?"

Novák's face was blank. "We're at war, Mr. MacCarthy. Extreme measures can only be met with extreme measures."

"You can't send him to Forest Hill," Terje said. "It's too dangerous."

"I think that's up to Lord Aviemore to decide."

Terje looked at me. His eyes shone with something, but they were too remote for me to figure out what. Whatever it was, it set unease rippling over my skin.

"Won't they know?"

"Know what?" Novák asked.

"Won't they be able to...smell you? Smell your Blood? In me?"

There was an uncomfortable silence, which Novák eventually broke. "The compound Terje has been taking suppresses his Blood's capacity to be detected. Assuming you haven't been taking too much —"

"He hasn't," Terje put in. It may have been the uncertain light, but for a moment I could swear he was blushing.

"Then it shouldn't be a problem," Novák finished.

"If I agree to this..." Terje started to interrupt me but I spoke over him, "*If...* Does this mean Terje is taken off Evgeniya detail?"

"Yes," Novák said.

"And what is his 'other task'?"

"I need someone to get close to these two," he said, nodding at the screen showing the Brassingtons getting into a chauffeured car, "and their associates. The money from their campaign is coming from somewhere. Some of their donors are public, like Jon Ogdell" — my stomach dipped, but Novák continued — "but there are plenty who aren't. And I've exhausted all my...legal...avenues for finding out who is funding them."

"Hire a private detective."

"I can do more than a human agent can," Terje said, not breaking eye contact with Novák.

"They're toffs," I scoffed. "They don't need anyone else's money to be wankers."

"The Brassington estate has been in debt for years. In the millions," Novák said, moving back to the sideboard and pouring more drinks, "until recently. It can't be a coincidence that their fervor for this cause has increased along with their bank balance."

I took the offered whiskey glass and stared into it without drinking. "You think there's something else going on?"

"There's *always* something else going on," Novák said. "And the current situation provides unique opportunities for anyone wishing to gain public support...for whatever reason."

I raised my eyebrows. "You think they have their eyes on Number 10?"

"Probably that...and more," Novák murmured. "Neither do I think it's a coincidence that their campaign has gained momentum since Evgeniya returned."

I frowned. "You think it's all linked?"

"I do."

"How can it be? They're *anti*-haemophile campaigners."

"It's not all clear. But whatever it is these people want, they are all prepared to do untold, perhaps irreparable damage to the perception of haemophiles to achieve it." He held out a glass of blood to Terje. "And I won't let that happen."

Terje took the glass and emptied it, not meeting my look.

"We're not going to be able to go back, are we?" I murmured, a horrible thought occuring. "To Glenroe?"

"What makes you say that?" Novák asked.

"Surely that's the first place Evgeniya would go, if she's after us?"

"Glenroe is safe."

"How?"

"I have it...patrolled," he said, not meeting my eye.

"What do you mean?"

"It is guarded. It's probably the safest place for you."

I stared. "There was someone in the caves. The builder heard them."

Novák sipped his drink. "That was probably her. She was supposed to remain undetected, but she has to rest somewhere."

"Who?"

"She is there to protect you," Novák said firmly. "You don't need to know any more. Just know that if you do what I ask of you, you'll both be able to return and be safe. Terje is right when he says this is everyone's fight, my lord. But I wouldn't ask you to join it if I couldn't protect you."

Terje met my eyes. I wished he would say something, tell me what he wanted. But they were both waiting for me.

"I'll do it," I said. "If it means our part in it will be over quicker, I'll do it."

Terje blinked, and I wondered what he was seeing in my face. Then we all drank and Novák smiled, revealing teeth like a lion's.

"My endless gratitude, as always," he said, reaching into his pocket and holding out an envelope and a glass vial to me. The vial was filled with black-red Blood, thick as cream.

"What's this?"

"Information on and directions to Forest Hill," Novák said, "and my Blood. You might need it to enter. And it will protect you while you're there."

"I thought you said they wouldn't talk to one of your representatives?"

"You're representing yourself," he replied. "This is just to get you in the door and ensure your safety."

I took the vial and put it in my pocket. It was uncomfortably heavy.

Terje and Novák switched to Norwegian, I guessed to discuss details of his own task they didn't think I needed to know. I finished my whiskey and stared at the floor. Finally, we were heading for the lift together.

"You shouldn't have mentioned that I give you my Blood," he murmured after the silence had stretched on for several moments. "That's private."

Annoyance rode up my spine. "How am I supposed to know these things if you don't tell me?"

"I thought you understood about that."

"Well, clearly you thought wrong."

Terje didn't reply.

"Do you even want to live with me?" I blurted.

He frowned. "What?"

"Just hearing you talk…and the way Novák talks… Hell, the people at Forest Hill are still thinking of Evgeniya as their Magister, even after everything she's done? Is there any chance for us, Terje? Can you ever leave it behind?"

His expression looked pained. His hesitancy in replying filled my belly with a dread, but then he threaded his fingers through my hair and drew my face to his. He swept his tongue into my mouth, deep but gentle. My knees went weak. I wanted to push him against the wall and show him just how much he meant to me, how much I wanted to know him, but he broke away and laid a hand on my face. "You are what's important to me, Alec."

"I'm really struggling to believe that right now…" I said, voice heavy with emotion.

He gazed at me for a long moment then leaned in and kissed me again, slow, tender. "You have no idea how wonderful you are," he said between kisses. "Your passion. Your pain. Even your anger. You overflow with it all. It's like heat. Like…lightning before a storm. It's…intoxicating. I want it. Want you — to be with you, more than I've ever wanted to be with anyone else."

My heart fluttered, my pulse thumping in my wrists and neck. I swallowed, tasting the ghost of his Blood on my tongue, and he smiled like he guessed my thoughts.

"I want all that, Alec. They just…won't let me. Not yet." He released me. "We just need to be patient."

"Easy for you to say," I muttered. "You're going to live forever."

He gave a half-smile. "Is that supposed to be a joke?"

"Maybe."

He squeezed my hand and his eyes warmed. The lift doors opened, and we were back in the carpark. We moved to the Jaguar and Terje got his bag out of the boot.

"So what happens now?"

"You go find yourself a hotel…unless you want to stay here?"

"Is *that* supposed to be a joke?"

"You just seem to enjoy Novák's company so much," Terje murmured, dark humor dancing in his eyes.

"It's like being in a room with a nuclear reactor," I muttered, and Terje smiled. "Yeah, I'll find a hotel, then tomorrow I'll go to this damn commune and see what they'll tell me. Or won't. What about you?"

"I'll do as Novák says—get close to those humans, see what I can find out."

"And you really think I'll be able to just walk into Forest Hill, no questions asked?"

"Novák's Blood will gain you entry. After that, it's up to you. You want to know where Evgeniya is, right? What she's planning?"

"Only so we can protect ourselves."

"That's all anyone will expect," he said. He threw me the keys. "You take the car. I won't need it. But, Alec," he paused, his face serious, "they're not all like me. Be careful."

"I will if you will."

He nodded. "I promise. And remember, you won't get a very friendly welcome before sunset."

"And I'll get a friendly welcome after, will I?" I said dubiously.

"Friendli*er*," Terje said with a shrug. There was a brittleness to his expression that made me uneasy.

"*Do* you miss them? Your own kind? Be honest. Please."

"Sometimes," was his reply, the word toneless. "You miss your family too, yes?"

I frowned. "Dad?"

Terje shrugged a shoulder again. "Maybe not him."

"Then who?"

"Megan. David. Your mother?"

I went still. "Why would you say that?"

Terje looked surprised. "You're only human, Alec."

Only human. I unlocked the car and looked back to say goodbye, but he was gone.

It was after midnight by the time I was slipping a keycard into the door of an anonymous chain hotel room somewhere in Islington. I lay on the bed and stared at the ceiling. It was ticking toward one a.m., but now I wasn't tired. I looked at my phone. No messages. Out of nowhere, the idea to phone Jay popped into my head. I disregarded it before it had fully formed, but not before guilt had prickled across my skin.

Next, Terje's words about family still fresh, I thought about phoning Meg, now living in North London. But what would I say?

"Sorry I never called you. Sorry I almost got you killed then abandoned you. Sorry I pretended not to know how you felt. How's tricks?"

I turned my phone face-down on the bedside table.

When sunrise lightened the edge of the blinds, I finally accepted that sleep was not going to come. I ordered a coffee to go from the hotel restaurant, climbed into the car and made for Hampstead.

The drive took over an hour, despite it being before six a.m. Horns blared, and motorbikes, pushbikes and scooters zoomed past with inches to spare. The pavements were thronging with people, sweating in their hurry to get somewhere. The heat of the morning was already strong, and I grew more certain with every sluggish mile that I was making a mistake. But I didn't turn back.

Meg and her husband lived in a handsome townhouse overlooking Hampstead Heath. I had never visited before, but she'd given me the address in one of the last conversations we'd had. I parked down the street. It was some time before I could make myself get out of the car. I told myself it was too early, too sudden, too rude even, to just turn up like this. But Terje's words had forced me to admit that I hadn't been able to stop thinking about her since that last text message. She was also the one person in the whole world with whom I might be able to talk about what was going on. It was a supremely selfish reason for seeking her out now, but I told myself at least it was a reason.

I climbed the steps to the front door, rubbed the back of my neck, glanced along the bright, leafy street then, finally, pushed the bell.

Nothing.

I shifted from one foot to another. A group of school children shrieked as they ran by, a tired-looking mother hurrying to keep up while pushing a pram. I pressed the bell again. Other people passed on bikes, and black cabs and cars trundled up and down the residential street as the minutes ticked by. I was about to give up when instinct made me push the bell a third time.

The lock clicked and the door was opened by a tall, dark-haired man, clean shaven but with dark circles under his eyes. He was in shirtsleeves, a somber tie slung, undone, under his collar.

"Yes?" he started, but then his expression flattened. "MacCarthy?"

"Uh, hi. Is Meg in?"

"It's half six in the fucking morning."

"I'm sorry. I won't be long."

The man scowled. "You've got a bloody nerve, showing up here."

"Look… I just want to see her."

"Tough shit. She's not here."

I took a breath, keeping my voice neutral with an effort. "Do you know when she'll be back?"

"Not a fucking clue. The bitch is gone. Good riddance."

I stared at him. His eyes shone with pain. He gripped the door with a white-knuckled hand. "What happened?"

"None of your damn business."

"Please. Brian, isn't it?"

"So she bothered to tell you my name, did she?"

"Of course she did," I said, my voice low.

"Will miracles never cease?"

I bit back my first response. "I just want to make sure she's okay."

"Well, I can't help you."

"You don't have any idea where she might be?"

"Don't know and don't care."

"When did she leave?"

He made an impatient noise. "A week ago. Why?"

I went cold. "She tried to get in touch with me recently."

"Of course. She'd rather talk to you than her own husband."

"I haven't done anything."

"No. You haven't, have you?"

The burn of his hate rolled over me like fire. "What happened, Brian?"

"She left me, that's what. Left me for someone else."

"Who?"

"How the fuck should I know?"

"Well, if you don't know who, how do you know she — ?"

"Texts. Phone calls. Late nights. She said it was work, but she's a shit liar." His face twisted, and for a horrible moment, I was certain he was going to cry, but then he drew himself up and continued. "Is that it, Lord Arsehole? Some of us have to work for a living, you know."

"This isn't right," I shook my head. "This isn't Meg."

"You obviously know her better than me," he said, and slammed the door.

I returned to the car in a daze, pulling my phone out as I went. I tried to call her. The phone went straight to voicemail.

"Meg, it's Alec. Ring me." It sounded terse, even to me, but I was annoyed…and scared…and annoyed that I was scared.

I tried to ring the unknown number she'd texted me from. Still nothing—and this contact number had no voicemail.

I selected another name in my phone book, chewed the inside of my lip as I prevaricated, then pressed the green call button. David's phone rang six times, then it, too, went to voicemail. I swore, unable to think of anything that could be said in a message, and hung up.

I left the car and wandered up the street, trying to think. My mind was fuzzy, both from my disrupted sleep and the emotional and information overload of the last few days. I made for the nearest café, ordered an espresso and chose a table at the back. I sipped the coffee, willing it to sharpen my mind, and started scouring Meg's social media profiles. She hadn't posted anything except business updates on her professional Twitter account for months. There was certainly no evidence of any affair, but there wasn't much evidence of anything at all. With a pang, I wondered what she'd been up to all this time besides falling out with her husband.

I shook my head and tried to ring her again. It still went straight to voicemail.

"Alec?" I started. Jay was standing by my table, grinning from ear to ear. "Bloody hell, lightning really does strike twice. What are you doing here?"

I blinked, trying to make my brain shift gears. He had his leather satchel on one shoulder and another short-sleeved polo-neck shirt on under a light jacket. The white cotton of his top pulled tight over his sculpted chest and stomach, and his skinny jeans didn't do much to hide the rest of him. I dragged my focus back to his face. "Uh…nothing. Just, I was in the area. What are *you* doing here?"

His eyes flickered and I wondered if my tone had offended him, but then he sat, beaming. "I've got a breakfast meeting around the corner in an hour. I came in to get fueled up. You got time for another?"

A nervous tickling started in my belly, but I said, "Yeah…sure."

Chapter Five

"So, what are you doing in London?" Jay asked as he sipped his drink. "Not that it isn't great to see you." He added it with such a loaded look that the squirming in my belly started all over again. "But I always thought it would take more than wild horses to drag you this far south."

"I... Nothing, really," I said, stirring my coffee to avoid his eye. "I, well...I have some business."

"You should have let me know. I could have put you up."

"I have a hotel," I said, a little too quickly. "It's fine, really."

He shrugged out of his jacket. I looked away from his toned arms as he rested them on the table. "What sort of business?"

I stirred more milk into my coffee to buy time. Then I sighed, suddenly fed up of lies. "Ivor Novák has asked me to do something for him."

Jay lowered his coffee cup and stared. "*The* Ivor Novák?"

"Yeah."

"What does he want with you?"

I sipped my drink, trying to unstick my dry mouth. "He wants me to visit Terje's old commune. I'm heading out tonight."

"Forest Hill?"

I frowned. "You've heard of it?"

He shrugged. "Everyone's heard of it." It was my turn to blink. "Why is he sending you there?"

"He thinks I might be able to find out if anyone has spoken to Magister Evgeniya."

Jay went white. "So the rumor's true? She's in the country?"

"They think so, yeah."

"Jesus, Alec. You gotta be careful. She's dangerous."

"I am aware."

"I'm serious. She's not like a lot of the others. She won't think twice about hurting you...or worse."

"Yes, I know," I insisted. "That's why I have to help Novák find her before she finds me."

Jay sat back in his chair, staring at me. "This is amazing, Alec."

"Not the word I would choose."

"No, you don't understand. You getting involved, I mean. Alec MacCarthy visiting Forest Hill is, well...huge."

"No, it isn't," I said firmly. "You can't tell anyone. I'm only telling you because you're one of the few people who would understand."

"But, Alec, if we made it known that you were reaching out to the haemophile community... That you, a human and a victim, were working with Novák and the haemophiles to protect everyone..."

"I'm not a social warrior, Jay. I'm just trying to live my life."

Jay sighed deeply but then leaned on his elbows, smiling at me through the stylish sweep of his hair. "I think you're missing out on a great opportunity. But of course I understand. Okay, so we don't tell anyone. Can I at least come along?"

"Come along? What for?"

"I can help."

"How?"

"I've met some of the commune residents before."

"You have?"

"Sure," he said with a shrug. "Some of them agreed to interviews. They're an important part of my book. Plus, I *know* about haemophiles, Alec—how they act, how they think. I can help you get the answers you need."

"Why would you do that?"

"Because it's important that Evgeniya Morak is caught before she has a chance to hurt anyone else. And, well"—he reached out and put his hand on my arm—"because it's important to you."

His hand was so warm that I resisted pulling away. "Thanks. It'd be good to have someone there. I'm not looking forward to it."

"Of course not," Jay said, drawing his dark eyebrows together. "It must so painful to meet Terje's commune now, like this. Novák shouldn't have asked it of you."

"He thinks I'm the only one with a chance of getting any answers."

"Well, he's probably right. You were Terje's partner. You have a right to try to find out if you're in any danger because of his ex-Magister. And the commune will understand that, to a point. But it's still a risk. He shouldn't have sent you there alone, without one of his people for protection, at least."

"He gave me this," I said, pulling the vial out of my pocket.

Jay's face slackened. "Is that...?"

"Novák's Blood, yeah."

Jay's gaze remained fixed on the bottle. "That's... Wow."

I frowned. "What's the big deal?"

"It's *Blood*, Alec," Jay said, a little breathlessly. "Capital 'B'? You know what the big deal is."

My cheeks warmed. "I'm not going to...*take* it. It's not for that. It's just so they know he sent me."

"It's more than that. Way more."

"What do you mean?"

"Haemophiles don't just give Blood away, Alec," he said. "It's a tremendous act of trust. Their Blood is their life — their existence, their protection and the essence of who they are. It's how they identify and track each other. And it's...powerful. Powerful in ways even they don't fully understand."

I pocketed the vial, suddenly uncomfortable.

Jay leaned close and spoke in a low voice. "You've...you've tried it, right?"

I blinked. "Blood?"

Jay nodded, seeming slightly feverish. "Not from a dealer, I mean. I mean consensually from...from him." He watched my face and blushed. I cursed myself that his reaction just intensified my own. "Sorry. That's such a personal question." He dropped his gaze to the table and lifted his coffee cup with trembling hands. When he lowered it again, he appeared calmer, but he still didn't look at me.

"I take it you've had it then?" I asked. He blushed harder, his caramel skin turning a deep pink. "It's dangerous, you know," I murmured, seeing how tightly he gripped his mug. "Addictive."

"It can be," he answered quietly. "People ruin their lives for it. And the black market is detestable as well as terrifying. But being given it in moderation by a willing partner...it's safe and, well..." He blinked rapidly and smiled again, though it was a little strained. "Sorry. Not appropriate. I just don't know many other people who've done it."

"You've had it from a partner?" I asked slowly.

He nodded. "There's nothing else like it, right?"

I glanced around, not sure what to think or feel.

"It's not just the physical effect," he went on in a hushed voice. "Though that's...well—" He laughed nervously then cleared his throat. "Yeah. Intense. But it's not just that. It's the act of trust. The bond it creates. It's not something you can experience with another human. And they so rarely pair with humans..." Jay's face was serious. "You were very lucky, Alec, to have what you had, even for a short time."

"Do you still...have it?" I asked after a long moment of silence.

Jay looked down at the table. "We..." Jay sniffed, scrubbed at his face. "I've not seen him in a while."

"I'm sorry."

"Don't be," he eventually replied. "He wasn't... I wasn't..." He coughed. "It's complicated. But forget it. It's not relevant. You're here now, and that's what's important." He caught sight of his watch and swore. "Crap, I'm late. But I'll see you later, yeah? You wanna head out there tonight?"

"Yeah, thanks."

"I'll pick you up at your hotel. Text me the address."

"Do you want the directions?" I said, fumbling for Novák's envelope.

"It's all right. I know the way," he said, standing and shouldering his bag. "Thanks, Alec. You won't regret this."

I was already doubting that as Jay hurried from the café, anticipation evident in every line of his toned body.

I decided to walk back to the hotel and return for the car later, hoping it might give my riotous thoughts a chance to calm. The day was heating up, the dull, hot sky cloudless above. I stripped out of my jacket and wove along the busy pavements, breathing in the strong city smells and regretting my decision. I was somewhere between Kentish Town and Islington when I finally stopped and scoured the traffic for a black cab. I was just lifting my hand to hail one when a large black saloon pulled up at the curb. I frowned as a big man in a dark suit climbed out of the passenger seat. He wore sunglasses and had the blank, anonymous look of private security. That and the glimpse of the gun I'd seen as he buttoned his jacket made me start scanning the busy street for possible escape routes.

"Lord Aviemore?" the man said in a cockney drawl.

"Who are you?"

"Mr. Smith, sir," he said with a blank smile. "Pleased to make your acquaintance. He opened the back door of the car. "If you'd like to come with us now, sir."

"Why?"

"Your presence is requested."

My palms began to itch. "By who?"

"That should be 'whom' there, sir." The man grinned. "And let's just say…an anonymous well-wisher."

"And why do they feel the need to be anonymous?"

"All your questions will be answered, sir. If you'd just like to get in, we can be on our way."

I turned away only to find another suited man standing behind me with the very obvious bulge of a shoulder holster under his jacket. He held out his hand.

"Phone," he grunted.

"Let's not make this hard, sir," Smith said.

My silent companion didn't even look at me.

"I don't respond well to threats."

"No, sir. Your criminal record is evidence of that." The second man's voice was deep and gravelly, the voice of someone who smoked fifty a day.

"Who are you? What is this?"

But the man said no more.

The journey felt like it took an hour, but my watch told me it was only a little over twenty minutes before the car tilted, like it was going down a ramp and the already-dim interior darkened even further. The car stopped and the door was opened. The two men escorted me across an empty, windowless car park, through a door they accessed with keycards and codes then along an anonymous, white-painted corridor. I looked around for anything to help me identify where I was, but there were no windows, the only light from LED spotlights in the ceiling.

They stopped outside another door, opened it with more codes and ushered me through. I blinked both in the sudden, warm light from a number of lamps and at the opulence of the room. The ceiling was high, and the walls covered in damask wallpaper. The floor space was crowded with large sofas and armchairs, carved coffee and side tables holding ornaments and framed photographs and, at the far end, a long walnut dining table that was polished to a mirror-like shine and surrounded by high-backed chairs. Tall bookshelves crammed with books filled the walls, and whatever leftover space was hung with oil paintings of people in stiff-necked collars and ruffs. It was like I'd stepped into the drawing room of a wealthy family's stately home...apart from the fact that there were no windows.

The two black-suited men took up positions inside the door. The only other people in the room were an older couple, a man and a woman, seated at the end of the large table surrounded by papers, laptops and open briefcases overflowing with files. They rose at my entrance, both wearing the exact same pinned-in-place smile that I recognized from a hundred formal gatherings of my youth — the smile of someone who is pleased about something but not about meeting you.

"Lord Aviemore," the woman cooed, her cut-glass English accent all at once conciliatory and deeply patronizing. "How good of you to join us."

"You want to tell me why I'm here?"

"Straight to the point," the man said, thumbs in his belt, sticking out his ample belly. "I like that. Not something you normally see in the aristocracy."

"I'm not—"

"Please, Lord Aviemore," the woman simpered, gesturing at a free chair, "have a seat. You're not in any danger. We just want a few moments of your time."

"So why the goons?"

The man glanced at the woman, who tilted her head and looked at me from under lowered eyebrows. "We have been very keen to talk to you for some time but, unfortunately, our attempts to make contact at your home have been...thwarted."

"What are you talking about?"

She went on like I hadn't spoken. "So, naturally, when we heard you were in London, we couldn't let the opportunity pass. But we assumed — correctly, it would seem — that you might be...reluctant to talk to us."

"So, politicians are really only obtuse when it suits them?"

Something flickered in their eyes, but they were both far too well-practiced at this to let anything more show on their faces. The woman indicated the chair again. "The sooner you listen to what we have to say, the sooner you can leave."

I glanced toward the heavies at the door again, then reluctantly took the offered seat. The pair resumed their own, sitting straight-backed and attentive, their hands clasped on the table like they were addressing another press conference. The woman pressed a buzzer and requested tea from an unseen menial, then refocused on me.

"Now, my lord, we have been most remiss. Allow me, first, to introduce ourselves."

"I know who you are."

Allegra Brassington watched me without moving. Edgar glanced between us with the air of a spectator watching a boxing match. "Yes, of course. I should have known that you couldn't be completely ignorant of current affairs." She smiled wider, the skin on her face thin and pale as it stretched around her too-white teeth. "For which I am glad. This will make this all the easier."

"Make *what* easier?"

A door opened and in walked a woman in a somber suit bearing a silver tea tray. She laid it on the table at my elbow, curtsied and left. Allegra reached for the gilded teapot. "Earl Grey, my lord?"

"I don't want tea," I said, curling my hand into a fist. "I want you to get to the point."

Allegra pointedly poured tea into two of the three cups, splashed in a little milk, held one out to her husband and took the other herself.

"The milk goes in first, you know," I muttered.

Allegra sipped her drink and I fought with every ounce of my strength to hold still. I knew this game. I remembered it from dinners at Cambridge and the endless evenings spent at Glenroe with Dad's barrister associates and fellow judges, everyone drawing out discussion about one thing when really they were angling for information about another. I knew how to play. Let the other party talk on until they had run out of bullshit so only the truth remained, even if it was the only thing left unsaid.

I waited.

Allegra set her cup in its saucer while Edgar continued to watch me, his own tea untasted.

"No doubt you are surprised by all this, Lord Aviemore," Allegra went on, "given our obvious differences of opinion on, probably, many things."

"You want something."

"How astute of you," she smiled. "Though you are mistaken in thinking this is something we want *from* you. It's more like something we want to do *for* you."

"And what's that?"

"We want to give you what you want, old chap," Edgar said, his voice thick and rolling like over-seasoned gravy.

"How could you possibly know what I want?"

"Because you want what we all want," Allegra said, spreading her hands, "your life back and made private again, your name and your home no longer linked to any scandal."

I narrowed my eyes. "And how can you do that?"

"Oh, a few ways," she went on, dropping a lump of sugar into her tea and stirring it with a silver teaspoon. "We can provide you with a new home, away from that drafty, damp monstrosity."

"Glenroe is not for sale."

"Oh, we don't want to buy it," she went on, mock surprise widening her watery eyes. "Heavens, no. I imagine the place is only fit for non-humans and, well...we are in the process of stopping non-humans from occupying anything but the strictest, most tightly surveilled habitations. No, you can keep Glenroe, if you really want to. But we will provide you with somewhere else to live, somewhere...private, where no one else would think to find you and where you would be protected."

"What if I don't want to move?"

"That's entirely up to you," she went on, sipping her tea with a smile. "But you're a clever young man. You have to see you cannot have the life you want in a place now so well-known. The isolation will only help you so much."

Something unpleasant uncoiled in my belly. "What, exactly, are you saying here?"

"I'm *saying*," she said, setting her cup down with a gentle click, "that we can guarantee you a better, safer, quieter and more private life. We can give you what you want. What *both* of you want."

A chill went up my back. "What do you mean, 'both'?"

"We're not here to make judgments," Allegra went on, her tone sickly-sweet. "It's true that my husband

and I are not in the position to fully understand your...predilections. But we also understand that what one can't change, one must accept. We don't believe you and your haemophile *partner* are a danger to anyone, otherwise this would be a very different conversation. But as you are clearly not—"

"Wait—"

She went on like I hadn't spoken, "We are more than willing to come to an arrangement that will suit you both, keep you safe and removed from all this mess."

I blinked, trying to make sense of what she was saying. "*How* exactly would you do that? And why?"

"The 'how' is easy," she said. "We have an associate in Scotland. They're already in the process of setting up a new home for you, somewhere that you and Terje Kristiansen can be safe and happy and live out your lives together."

My hand curled into a fist. "Terje is dead."

She gave me a frank look. "It is our job to know things most people don't, my lord, so let's not be foolish and try to lie. As to the 'why' you mentioned? Well..." She glanced at her husband with raised eyebrows. Edgar raised his own in return, then she looked back to me. "It suits all of us to have you out of the way. We understand *your* part in the Blood Winter conspiracy, young man. But Rådgiver Novák must be stopped. His keeping of secrets and relying on his own authority to solve problems caused those unfortunate events, not to mention the faking of Mr. Kristiansen's death to gain publicity."

"How do you—?"

"These details are unimportant. What is important is that it's simply best all-around if you are kept away from it all. Then you cannot be used again. And we, well" — she poured herself more tea — "we have the advantage of revealing the truth about what Novák did while knowing that you and Mr. Kristiansen will not come to any further harm because of it."

"You mean if we're out of the way and owe you, we can't speak out against you?"

She sighed, looking faintly disappointed. "Do you really want to?"

I glared at the tea tray.

"There, see?" Edgar said. "We knew you'd understand. We both want the same things in the end, old boy. You and your, uh, *boyfriend* out of the way, somewhere pleasant and safe, living your own lives quietly and privately. Leave the bigger picture to us."

I stared at the tray a moment longer before fire lit along my veins. I was furious with myself that I'd started to consider it.

"You can get to fuck, the pair of you," I said, standing and heading for the door, but the heavies stepped into my path. "I suggest you move."

"We're just asking you to think about it," Allegra said, rising. "We want the same things you do, my lord. It may be for different reasons, but doesn't the end justify the means?"

"*Move*," I repeated.

The men looked up and Allegra nodded. They opened the door and followed me down the corridor and back to the car park. I tried to find a door, but instead they opened the car.

"Just let me out."

"Orders, sir," the cockney said, without any apology in his tone.

I ground my teeth and climbed in. I chafed and fidgeted for the whole drive which, again, felt far longer than it was.

When they finally stopped, I got out to find we were outside my hotel. I glared as the man returned my phone, then the dark car was disappearing into traffic.

I hurried to my room, ringing Terje as I went. I knew he wouldn't answer in the middle of the day, but I just prayed he'd check his messages as soon as he was awake.

When it went through to the answerphone, I tried to talk calmly. I told him what had happened, that the Brassingtons knew he was alive and that they had a plan to get us out of the way. I also told him they were following me and that I knew me turning them down wouldn't be the end of it.

"Be careful," I said as my rambling message drew to a close. "Please."

I sat on the bed, staring at the wall, trying to decide if I should leave a message for Novák as well. But I rubbed my eyes, suddenly exhausted. Terje would tell him if he needed to know — if he didn't have spies on hand who would tell him anyway. I never put anything past Novák, knowing he saw us all as pieces in a game that was far beyond my understanding.

I was so fed up with being a playing piece. And I was suddenly very tired of Terje continuing to allow them to use us that way.

Jay's smiling face came back to me and I was suddenly tempted to give him his interview, to take the chance to get our side of the story out there. He had his own reasons too, but I realized that I believed what he said, about his coming from a sincere desire to make things better.

It was easy to say no to being involved to Novák…to the Brassingtons. It was harder saying no to Jay, harder than even saying it to Terje.

And that worried me.

But I shook my head. Giving an interview wouldn't change anything, whatever Jay thought. If anything, it could make things worse. Once the words were out there, they could be misconstrued, misquoted, twisted to imply anything anyone with an agenda wanted.

Living through the downfall of Judge MacCarthy had shown me that.

I slept through most of the afternoon, then woke with an aching erection. I slipped my hand into my pants but stopped, remembering that the dream I'd woken from hadn't been about Terje. I stared at the ceiling, breathing until the arousal subsided, then pushed back the covers, damning Jay and myself before stepping into a cold shower.

I tried to reach Terje again as soon as night fell. Still, he didn't answer. I cursed. Surely me getting abducted would be something he'd want to talk to me about? I shook my head and was just pocketing my phone when a message pinged in from Jay.

I'm outside.

I took a deep breath, stared at the carpet until I had my racing thoughts under control, then I replied.

On my way.

Jay kept up mindless, friendly chatter on the two-hour drive to Forest Hill and, as the miles stretched on, I found I was enjoying myself. Jay was as easygoing and carefree as he had been at university, despite everything he'd been through. And it was nice to speak to someone who remembered the good times from Cambridge and not just the train wrecks that were my relationships with David and my father. I had thought they defined those years, the bad times permeating and staining every memory like spilled ink. But reminiscing with Jay about the nights out, the music we'd discovered together, the people we'd known, the places we'd gone hiking and climbing, it suddenly occurred to me that perhaps they didn't have to.

I pondered telling him about the Brassingtons but decided that there already too many lies to keep track of, so I kept quiet and let him talk.

The busy streets of London gradually gave way to emptier roads. The crush of buildings thinned, and the suburbs and outlying districts began to break up. The night wore on and, eventually, we pulled off a dual carriageway onto a winding country road. There were no signs, but Jay made his unerring way along the narrow road and turned onto another, even smaller track and stopped outside a pair of large, steel gates. There was no sign, and whatever lay beyond the pool of the illumination from the headlights was lost in the darkness.

"Are you sure this is it?"

"This is it all right," Jay said. His face was serious, possibly even a little scared. "I've been to the gates before, but never been let in. My interviews happened at my flat."

"Do we push a bell or something?"

"No."

"So what do we do?"

"We wait."

"How will they know we're here?"

"They already know we're here," he replied and turned the headlights off.

I stared out into the dark, broken only by the cool, white sparks of the stars overhead. "I'm not sure this was such a good idea," I murmured.

"We'll be fine," Jay said. "Remember… They don't want to hurt us. Not this commune, anyway. But they won't trust us, either."

"I don't even know what I'm going to say."

"Just be honest," Jay said. "They can read us very easily. There's no point in lying. But why would you want to?"

I swallowed. My palms started to sweat. "What are they like? The communes?"

Jay shrugged. "They're all different. This one is built into the foundations of an old stately home. There's not much left above ground. But information about their location and layouts is protected, so you never know what they're going to be like. But I do know that at least thirty registered haemophiles live here."

"*Thirty?*"

Jay nodded. "The legal limit. Don't look so worried, Alec," he said with a smile. "They're a law-abiding commune. They live off donations. Evgeniya has harmed them more than anyone else, even you." His expression shifted. "I'm sorry. I know that's probably hard for you to believe, but most haemophiles just want to be left alone."

"I can understand *that*," I muttered, scanning the dark and fidgeting.

It was then that I realized someone was standing between us and the gate, their outline just visible in the starlight. I swore. Jay went still.

"Okay," he said quietly, "follow my lead."

I nodded but had to force myself to move when he opened his door. I climbed out into the warm night. The figure in the shadows was still as a statue. I got only the impression of pale skin and dark hair and clothes, but the glint of unblinking eyes was unmistakable.

Jay grabbed my sleeve to stop us several feet away.

"Good evening. My name's Jay Singh and this is Alec MacCarthy. He was hoping to be allowed in to speak with you."

Silence answered him. I held myself very still, my skin crawling while I tried to breathe normally.

"Alec MacCarthy." The voice that eventually came out of the dark was low, male and oddly accented, sounding like water over stones. "And what business do you have with us?"

"I just want to talk."

Silence again. Longer this time. "You knew Terje Kristiansen."

"That's right."

"This is about Magister Morak."

My blood slugged noisily in my ears. Jay's squeezed my shoulder. "Yes," he said.

"Novák sent you."

"He did," I said, even though it wasn't a question. I held out the vial, gratified that my hand didn't shake. The haemophile still didn't move, but the light in his eyes seemed to change.

"There is nothing we can do for you."

"I'm just asking for a few minutes," I said, "for Terje's sake." The emotion in my voice surprised even me. The silence that followed had a different quality. Eventually it was broken by something that might have been the haemophile equivalent of a sigh.

"Wait here," he said, then we were alone again.

"You did good," Jay said softly.

"If you say so," I said, wiping damp palms on my jeans.

"Magister Nordström will see you."

I jumped. The voice had come from my right. I blinked in the sudden light from an electric lantern.

"That's for us," Jay murmured.

I took the lantern from the haemophile and raised it. He was tall with close-cropped black hair over a long, almost vulpine face. Black eyes glinted in the low light, then he was gone. I lifted the lantern higher and saw that the gate stood open. I stepped through with Jay close behind and paced up the long, curving drive beyond. The night air still held some of the warmth of the day as well as the smell of trees and grass—and, under that, the subtle but distinct smell of rot and woodsmoke. I couldn't see any lighted windows or hear anything beyond our own footsteps. The haemophile kept ahead, just on the edge of the pool of light, moving without the slightest noise.

So quick that I almost lost him, he stepped off the drive onto a paved footpath across a neatly trimmed lawn. We hurried after him and soon there was a grating sound of a heavy door opening. We arrived at what looked like a concrete outbuilding. Its steel door, heavy with bolts and locks, was open.

"You ready?" Jay murmured. I took a steadying breath and nodded. "I'll go first."

We descended bare, concrete stairs. The air cooled rapidly. It was dark until we stepped off the last step into a bare, subterranean chamber with dim electric lights set in the wall on either side of a large door. The haemophile was there, tapping a code into a keypad then swiping a card through a reader. The heavy doors rumbled as they slid open.

"Quite the setup," I murmured.

"We do not encourage visitors," the haemophile replied.

Jay gave me a reassuring glance, then we followed the tall figure through the door.

Stepping from the utilitarian concrete stairwell into the well-appointed, if minimal, furnished lobby area was surreal, and I suppressed a shudder, reminded of my visit to the Brassingtons. Dim lamps in each corner provided some very low light. Simple but comfortable chairs were set against the walls. There was a large electric fire mounted on the wall to my right, the digital flames swaying dreamily in an imaginary wind. It warmed the high-ceilinged room to a comfortable temperature. There were framed photographs on the walls — landscapes, snow-capped mountains, rushing rivers and tall trees — countryside too dramatic to be the UK.

Our guide told us to wait and disappeared through another door. I caught a glimpse of a long, low-lit hallway before it hissed shut behind him. More locks clicked.

"You're doing great," Jay murmured, but he wasn't looking at me. He was staring around the room. I was staring at the camera lens in the corner of the ceiling.

"High security," I said.

"They have to protect themselves," Jay said, examining the photographs, "as well as humans stupid enough to try to break in during the day."

I remembered Terje's face when the Blood had taken control and suppressed another shiver.

The doors opened again. The black-haired haemophile returned with two more — both female, both taller than me, their limbs so long that they looked oddly angular. I was instantly reminded of Evgeniya and stiffened.

They were clad simply, jeans and neutral-colored shirts, no jewelry, no accessories. But their sharp-angled faces with deep, intense eyes were striking and terrifying enough to have the breath catching in my throat. The taller of the two had auburn hair pulled back in a braid that fell halfway down her back. Her eyes glowed like river ice on a winter's morning. The other's hair curled about her face, red as blood against her white skin. Her eyes were the sort of green I'd only ever seen in stained glass windows. They looked right through me.

"Mr. Singh," the taller of the two said in a flat, toneless voice, low for a woman, "how pleasant to see you again. Though I must confess I did not expect you here, unannounced."

Jay smiled a gracious smile. "Magister Nordström," he said, stepping forward. "Yes, I'm sorry for any inconvenience. This is Alec MacCarthy. He's a friend of mine."

"I'm well aware of who this is," she replied, sizing me up in a way that made me feel scrutinized and dismissed simultaneously. "Lord Aviemore, I am Hedda Nordström and this is my deputy, Ana Bonny. We thought you might call on us sometime and you are welcome, though it might have been wiser to arrange an appointment elsewhere. We're not really set up for your kind here...light, temperature, that sort of thing."

"It's fine," I said, my voice rough. "I just…" I glanced at Jay, who gave me an encouraging smile. "I was hoping to ask you something."

"Can I ask, why now?"

I blinked. "Sorry?"

"You want to know more about Terje." She gestured toward the circle of chairs near the fire. "I remember a little of human needs," she said, folding herself into one of the deep armchairs with the grace of a dancer. "And we are encouraged to communicate with those humans who wish to do so, but he's been gone nearly three years."

I sat and tried to think where to begin. Jay sat next to me, crossing his legs, seemingly at ease, but he was watching the haemophiles with an intensity that told me he was almost as on edge as I was.

"Magister," he said, "Alec and I have come to speak to you because we are…concerned."

"About what?" The red-haired haemophile put in, her voice fluting with a strong Romanian accent.

Jay looked at me. I took a breath, drew out the vial of Blood and put it on the table between us. "Ivor Novák asked me to come," I said. "I didn't want to. I didn't want to be involved. But I've been left without a choice."

"Is that right?" Nothing had changed in Nordström's face, but my muscles stiffened one by one under her gaze. "And if Rådgiver Novák has questions for us, why didn't he come himself?"

"He thought you would be more likely to talk to me."

"Why?"

"I don't know. Maybe because he is an outsider, but I once meant something to one of you."

Nordström didn't react, but Bonny tilted her head to one side. "They want to know if we've heard from Evgeniya, Magister," she said. "They think we might be plotting with her to wreak bloody revenge on those who brought about her downfall."

My palms prickled. Jay had gone very still. In the depths of Nordström's eyes, something stirred.

"That's not what we think," Jay said after a pause, his expression earnest.

"Mr. Singh," Nordström cut him off, "we have enjoyed a cordial relationship in the past. I thought you understood matters better than this."

"I do," Jay insisted. "We both do. We're trying to help."

"By accusing us of criminal activity in the same breath as asking me to betray my commune's confidences?"

"Please," Jay said, sitting forward, his face tense. "We understand Evgeniya Morak was once your Magister, but she betrayed all of you. She set your fight for acceptance back years—and she's likely to do it again."

"Evgeniya is no longer Magister of this commune," Nordström intoned. "She has no power here...no authority. You should know better than to suppose we would want to repeat her mistakes."

"We don't think that," I said, meeting her eye. "But I know what your bonds are like. You can't break them, even when you want to."

Nordström regarded me levelly. "That may be true, but it is more than our lives are worth to maintain links with Evgeniya Morak. The very least we could expect would be an army of humans with guns and nets and daylight floods. I would never do that to my commune."

"Of course not," I said, "but someone here may have heard from her? Helped her return, helped find her shelter?"

Nordström gave a low chuckle. "Son, none of us, least of all an elder, need any help to do that."

"You feel things," I said. "I know you do." Nordström blinked. The red-haired haemophile was very still. "You need each other. If Evgeniya is back, she will have reached out to someone."

Nordström hesitated the barest second then stated, "You're mistaken."

"So no one's seen her, spoken to her...*sensed* her?"

"We've sensed her. That's no secret."

Jay shifted in his chair. I swallowed and asked, "So, where is she?"

"It's not like GPS, my lord. I can't give you a postcode. But you should know," she added, her gaze sharpening, "that even if I did know, I wouldn't tell you. It's not personal. It's just not yours to know."

"But—"

"We take care of our own," Nordström cut him off. "If Evgeniya becomes a danger, we will handle it. Otherwise, none of it is human business. Now, is that all?"

"This woman has the power to ruin everything," I said in a hoarse voice. "If it were up to me, I would never even hear her name spoken. But I can't run from reality anymore."

Magister Nordström looked at me for such a long time that I thought she wasn't going to speak again. But then she leaned forward and put a heavy, long-fingered hand on my shoulder.

"I'm sorry about Terje," she said in a low voice. "We all are. And I'm sorry for your pain. But this isn't your business. The best thing for you to do is to return home and stay out of it. This will be resolved, but it will happen faster without interference."

"That's not true, Magister," Jay protested. "Haemophiles can't continue to solve these problems alone. We will be segregated forever if we carry on fighting our battles separately. You can trust us. Trust us to help."

"Write your book, Mr. Singh," Nordström said, standing. "Maybe it will change a few human minds for a while. That's better than nothing. But this world wore ruts for itself long ago. Some things are not meant to change." She nodded to us and moved toward the door. "Good luck to you both, sirs. Be careful out there."

She disappeared, followed by the black-haired male who had stood silent by the doors during the interview. We were alone with Ana Bonny, who hadn't once taken her eyes off me.

Chapter Six

"You were with him at the end, weren't you?" Bonny's accented voice was all at once ageless and light as a child's. Her glass-green eyes were large, fringed with thick lashes, strengthening the illusion of youth. But the years in their depths and the motionless, almost rigid way she held herself made me feel as though she was looking at an ancient painting.

"Yes. Yes, I was."

The faintest of lines appeared between her arching eyebrows. "Did he suffer?"

"Yes."

Bonny was silent for a long time then shifted forward in her chair, leaning close, staring at me. "He fought the Blood, didn't he? Let death take him rather than let it kill to survive?" Her eyes shone. I realized with a shock that there were tears in them.

"You knew him?"

She nodded. "I did."

Tendrils of something unpleasant wound their way around my spine. "I tried so hard to understand him. Now I'm wondering if I ever had a chance."

She glanced at Jay then back at me. "Can any living being truly know the truth of another?"

"What do you mean?"

"The gulf may be wider between our kinds," she murmured, "but it's the same darkness that lies between us all."

"Darkness?"

"The darkness of unknowing," she said softly, "of never being able to know... But in that darkness...that's where trust exists." She took my hand. Her flesh was cool and she was careful not to press her long, glass-like fingernails into my skin. "He trusted you, Alec MacCarthy — trusted your kind more than most of us do."

"What do you know about him?" I asked, shifting forward on my seat. "Where did he grow up? What was he like before?"

The start of a pained smile turned up the corner of her too-red mouth. "Darling, those aren't the important questions."

"They're not?"

"You're asking who he was when he was human?"

"I..." I glanced at Jay. He was watching me intently, but I turned back to Bonny. "I want to know."

"Why?"

"Because..." I took a breath. Her eyes stripped away my defenses and suddenly the truth was pouring out of me like blood from a wound. "Because I can't stop wondering whether it would have been better...whether I'd've been enough for him if he was human."

"But you wouldn't ever have met."

"I know it doesn't make sense—but I can't stop thinking about it."

"Poor darlings. You're all so young. You can never really understand. You don't live long enough."

"Do *you* know? What he was like before?"

She shook her head. "I joined this commune in the seventies. He'd been with them almost forty years by then. But our human lives had been around the same time, even though we'd never met then. So we grew close." Her gaze went far away, and I experienced a stab of jealousy. "I knew him well—but only as one of our own kind."

"And he never told you about his life when he was human?"

"We don't really remember the life before—not the way, say...humans remember their childhoods. It just...fades away. Some of us remember scraps, the ghosts of memories, of feelings. Some try to hold on. Some relish letting it go. But however we decide to feel about it, the Blood defines our existence. It's what makes us what we are, for better or worse." She stood. "I'm glad he had you, Alec MacCarthy," she said. "He was drawn to humans. But they rarely have the strength to cope with us...and vice versa." She threw Jay an intriguing smile. "It's why it's best if we keep apart, especially now that we're together...if you understand my meaning."

"So it was always doomed?"

Something like surprise flattened her face. "What do you mean?"

"Our relationship. Could a human and a haemophile ever be happy together?"

She looked at me so closely then that I was certain I'd given everything away. But then her soft smile was back, and the emerald of her eyes warmed to the color of summer grass. "Of course we can be happy...for a while. A long while, for your kind. Happiness in any partnership depends on our willingness to be happy with ourselves, with what we have...not yearning for what we don't." She sighed. "Humans know that in principle, but it takes a lot of practice to master, sometimes more than one lifetime's worth." She dimpled at Jay. "Some of you get closer than others, though. Terje seemed to be able to find those."

"I'm not sure I'm...was...anywhere near good enough at that to make it work..." I felt gutted, finally putting the fear into words.

"You might have been...one day."

Another stab through my chest. "He'd had relationships with humans before. Your ex-Magister told me that. And they didn't end well."

Her face hardened. "That's both right and wrong."

"That girl...Shelly...she died because of one of them."

Jay started. "Shelly Morris?"

I chewed on the inside of my cheek and kept my focus on Bonny. "I can't talk about that," she said in a low voice. "But it wasn't Terje's fault."

"Terje Kristiansen killed Shelly Morris?" Jay's face was stricken.

"No," I said, hurriedly. "No, he did not."

"Alec," he said breathlessly, "that murder is a major roadblock to progress. If you know the truth about it—"

"I don't," I insisted. "I really don't. I just know Terje didn't kill her..."

"What *do* you know?" Jay asked, his expression tight.

I swallowed. I couldn't read Bonny's face. "He blamed himself for it. But it wasn't him. It was another haemophile sent to follow him by Evgeniya, when she got suspicious of the human he was seeing…"

"Someone from Forest Hill?" Jay breathed.

"That's enough," Bonny cut in, voice firm. "I'm happy to talk to you about Terje, Alec — but not that."

I nodded, staring into the fire then jumped when she laid a hand on my arm. I could feel the strength in it, the prick of the claw-like fingernails through my jacket. She was so close that I could smell the heady, wine-like odor of her Blood in the air between us.

"I knew Terje well," she said softly. "Loved him, in a way — and he me. But what he felt for you was different, Alec." I met her green gaze with something both amazing and terrifying taking hold of my insides. "You might not be able to understand it…ever. But you can trust in it. I promise."

"Why are you doing this?"

"Doing what?"

"If you loved him…" Pain tightened my throat. She watched me steadily. "Why do you care about what he thought about me?"

"Because I cared for him. And knowing he had the potential to be happy is important to me…even if it killed him."

She squeezed my arm then turned to leave. Jay stood silent at my elbow, but I couldn't look at him.

Bonny paused at the door. "Oh and, just so you know, the Magister was telling the truth about Evgeniya, about her not being in contact with any of us. But that in itself should tell you something."

S. J. Coles

I blinked, my mind not wanting to switch focus.

"In what way?" Jay asked, frowning.

"We know she's...around." She made a vague gesture with her hand. "We know because she—how would you say it?—*passed by* several months ago. As in"—she frowned at the floor, as though searching for words—"she passed within, oh, maybe a hundred miles of here? We all felt it. But she didn't stop, and she didn't make contact." Her soft lips tightened. She looked at Jay. He was frowning.

"And that's significant?" I asked carefully.

"It's...unexpected," she said softly. "Hedda is right when she says Evgeniya wouldn't need our help, and neither would she willfully endanger us. But we've been together for hundreds of years, some of us. The fact that she passed us by without even a word?" Hurt brightened her eyes and she looked away. "It's telling."

"Of what?" I asked.

She tapped a code into the door pad and the doors slid open. "I don't know. But whatever she is planning, it doesn't involve us." The hurt was still evident in her childlike face. But then she blinked, and the emotion was gone. She nodded to each of us in turn. "Good luck to you both. Maybe we'll see you again. But perhaps ring ahead next time."

She winked, then she was gone.

* * * *

It started to drizzle as we made our way back to Jay's car. The drops were cool against my flushed skin. Jay left the lantern by the gate and we climbed into the car in silence. He steered along the country lanes without speaking. I stared out into the night, not even trying to untangle the wreath of emotions winding themselves around my heart.

"I'm sorry, Alec," Jay murmured when the orange of London's light pollution became visible as a stain on the horizon.

"What for?" I asked dully.

"That must have been hard."

I didn't answer and he said no more. The miles fell away, and soon the drizzle stopped and the western sky started to lighten. The next thing I knew, Jay had pulled over and turned off the engine. I blinked out at a large red-brick terrace.

"Where are we?"

"My place. I thought you could use a drink."

His smile was tinged with sadness. I was distantly aware that under other circumstances it would have annoyed me intensely. But in that moment, I found myself grateful for such a flawed, human display of emotion. He took in my expression and laid a hand on my knee.

I stared at it. Electricity rippled up my leg and lit in the dark hallow in my chest. The synthetic leather of the upholstery creaked as he leaned in and pressed a kiss against my cheek. He sighed into my ear. "Come up, just for a bit."

I followed him out of the car in a daze then up the steps to the front door. He put a key into the heavy lock then we climbed a set of stairs. He unlocked a door on the top floor and opened it into a dim, airy space with sloping ceilings, simple, comfortable furniture and tall casement windows looking out onto rooftops, glistening with the recent rain. He sat me on the sofa and brought me a glass of whiskey. It was a blend, but the heat and strong flavor were welcome and went some way to reviving the dullness that threatened to numb every inch of me.

"It was right, what Bonny said," he said softly, sitting beside me.

"What? That we can be happy with a haemophile so long as we're happy about what they can't give us?" I shook my head and downed the drink.

He pulled the empty glass from my fingers and set it on the coffee table. The low light bathed his skin. The color reminded me of fires and fertile earth, the shade of tree bark and strong, sweet tea. He locked his gaze on mine and it darkened, like ceramic fired in a kiln. He edged closer. His face was inches from mine, his aftershave a woody, natural scent. My mouth dried out.

"You're amazing, Alec," he murmured. "Everything you've been through, and yet here you are, still fighting, still wanting to understand." He trailed his thumb down the stubble on my cheek. I grabbed his hand. His flesh was so warm, his face so intent and his eyes fixed on mine. I could barely breathe.

He brought my hand to his face and brushed his lips over the knuckles. His breath, quickening, brushed over my skin. The hair on the backs of my hands rose. My heart thumped against my ribs. He raised his hot brown eyes to meet mine then turned our joined hands over and took my index finger into his mouth. I jolted, blood surging into my groin. The warm, moist wetness slid against my skin and the feel of his tongue looping around the sensitive pad had my breath catching in my throat. I closed my eyes, but it was no good. I could still feel it...feel him. How hot, how young...how alive. How unlike Terje.

I pulled my hand away, stood then stepped to the window.

"It's okay." Jay's voice was soft as he came up behind me. His firm chest and the hardness of his arousal pressed against my back. He slid a hand into my shirt. His breath was hot against my neck as he kissed my nape, more gently than a butterfly landing on the skin. "It's okay to be afraid, Alec. It's okay if you don't want to let go. I'm not asking you to. I just want to help you feel something different for a while."

He trailed his hand down my belly then slid it slowly into the front of my jeans. I inhaled sharply. He held me close, taking hold of my cock with one hand and sliding the other farther into my shirt to tease my nipples. They hardened and tingled under his touch. Fire and electricity built behind my ribs. It was a hot, sudden storm, so different without Blood, instantly urgent and clamoring to be sated.

I turned and shoved Jay against the wall. He moaned as I thrust my hips against his and my tongue into his mouth. He tasted like whiskey and warmth and human male. He hooked a leg around my thighs to draw me closer. The pressure was all at once delicious and maddening. I deepened the kiss, swallowing the taste of him, so different, so easy to understand...so easy to get lost in.

He pulled my shirt over my head, then his mouth was on my sternum. He licked my nipples, making me gasp as he undid the fly of my jeans.

"Jay," I started, but he kissed me again, taking the lead this time, thrusting his tongue into my mouth as if he would devour my protests. He backed me up until my legs hit the sofa, then pushed me onto it. He pulled his own shirt off and I just had time to register the scarring on his neck before he bent over me, kissing me and shoving my jeans down.

"You're gorgeous," he panted in my ear, taking my cock in his hand again. "So fucking gorgeous, Alec."

I tried to speak again, but all that came out was a low moan as he worked the hard flesh of my erection with skillful, eager hands. "Fuck, Jay," I breathed.

"Let go," he said, turning me so we lay on our sides, facing each other. "Just let go, Alec."

I crushed my eyes shut and grasped his hard cock where it rocked against my belly. He made a noise that had every inch of my flesh rippling. I sank myself into the feel, the smell and the sounds of his increasingly urgent need. I forced my eyes open so I could see him, see his flushed face, the sweat sticking his hair to his forehead. His eyes were closed, his mouth open. He looked amazing, loose, vulnerable and desperate.

I kissed him and he moaned my name against my lips. A charge was building like a thundercloud in my pelvis, and as his breathing caught in his throat, I knew he was close too.

"I want to taste you," I rasped.

He shot his eyes open. All he managed was a nod. I shifted down the sofa, pumping my own cock when it fell out of his reach, then took his slick, salty member into my mouth. I moaned at the heat, the living taste and smell sending answering jolts through my flesh.

"Alec," he warned. His head was thrown back against the sofa arm and he was digging his fingers into the cushions. "Alec, Jesus, I'm gonna —"

I sucked him hard and took him deeper, opening my jaw wide to allow him into my throat. He cried and his hips bucked as he thrust into my mouth. After he made a strangled sound, hot, salty fluid spurted onto the back of my tongue. I pumped my own cock once, twice more, then thunder and fire avalanched through my belly, down my legs and up my spine as I came.

* * * *

"You loved him, didn't you?"

I jerked from the warm, honey-colored stupor I'd been drifting in. Half-asleep, we'd cleaned up in the en suite then crawled into bed. I was on my back, Jay's head on my shoulder, his warm weight solid and comforting along my side.

I had successfully put off thinking until those words were out of his mouth. I now went cold, despite the warmth of the room and the naked body pressed against mine.

"I...I could have." The words croaked out of me as if they were being pried out with a crowbar.

Jay propped his head on his elbow and gazed into my face. "It won't hurt forever, Alec."

I swallowed, remembering when Novák had told me the same thing and thinking about how I was still, somehow, waiting for that to come true. I tentatively ran my fingers over the scarring on his neck. He didn't move, but his expression changed. "Did he do this to you?" I murmured. "Your haemophile partner?"

Jay gave me a crooked smile. "Well, it wasn't a human, was it?" he said, brushing his fingers over the similar marks on my own neck. "What about this?" he asked, softly.

"Evgeniya," I said, hoarsely and his expression darkened. "They're not supposed to do it. Even consensually."

"We're not supposed to drink theirs either," he said. "But you've done that. Right?"

"Yes…but them drinking from us is way more dangerous. It's too easy for them to get carried away."

"He told you that, did he?"

"Yes."

"So he never asked you…?"

"No," I said quickly. "I offered once. He was offended."

Jay shrugged a little awkwardly. "Some of them don't like it, especially the ones who have gone through a lot to ensure that direct feeding isn't necessary anymore. But between two willing partners? What's wrong with that?"

"It's dangerous," I repeated.

"Just *being* with one of them is dangerous, Alec. But that's what's so irresistible, right?" I couldn't find an answer to that. He smiled and pressed a kiss against my forehead. "Sleep. It's been a long night."

What had been a comfortable embrace now felt stiff and awkward. He must have sensed it too, because he rolled away from me. I listened to his breathing slow and level out as he drifted off, but it was a long time before sleep came for me.

* * * *

I woke to lamplight spilling in through the bedroom door, the smell of cooking spices and the sound of Jay moving around in the kitchen. For a blissful moment I didn't understand where I was, then it all came screaming back.

I fumbled my way across the room to the bathroom, locked the door behind me, leaned against it and covered my face with my hands until my pulse calmed. I made myself take a long, hot shower. But when I was done, I could still smell him on me, still taste him in my throat and still knew that I'd liked it.

I stared at the door, knowing I couldn't stay locked in forever but not quite able to move.

A knock on the wood made me jump.

"Alec? All okay in there?"

I hung my head, kneading my temples. "Yeah. Fine."

"Okay," Jay said uncertainly. "You hungry? I made breakfast…dinner, whatever."

I took a deep breath and opened the door, keeping my expression neutral. "Thanks. Sounds good."

Jay was smiling but his eyes were uneasy. Whatever he read in my face caused him to look away. Night had fallen outside, and Jay went around the living room drawing the blinds. I sat at a round table near the wall and he laid a cup of strong coffee and a plate of spiced potatoes, flatbread and homemade chutney in front of me. The smell was rich and made my belly clench with hunger, but it took a huge amount of effort to lift a forkful to my mouth.

"How are you doing?"

I chewed to delay answering. "Good." Jay watched me over the rim of his coffee mug. "You didn't need to do all this," I said, pronging another forkful.

"It's fine," he said, glancing at the clock, which read a little after eight p.m. "I usually get up around this time. It makes my work easier."

I nodded absently and drank some of the coffee. It was good and strong. I swallowed it greedily, willing it to jumpstart my reasoning.

"Look, Alec," Jay said, putting his mug down, "about yesterday…"

"You don't need to say anything."

"Shouldn't we talk about it?"

"Why?" He blinked at me. "Sorry. I'm not sure what you want me to say."

He sighed. "I don't want you to say anything. It's just that...it was good, I thought. *We* were good. I'm not attaching strings or anything." Jay shrugged and looked into his coffee. "It just felt like there was something there."

Heat flooded my face. I laid down my fork. "I just... It's not... It's complicated."

"I know it is," he said. "I understand. I do. But there's no harm in admitting you enjoyed it." His smile turned wolfish. "I think you did. Didn't you?"

"Of course."

"Well then," he said, turning his attention to his own plate, "we'll leave it there for now." He smiled to himself as he ate.

I finished my own food then retrieved my jacket from the back of the sofa.

"So, what now?" he said as he loaded dishes into his dishwasher.

"I need to speak to Novák, I guess," I said sullenly. "Tell him what Bonny said, which was basically nothing. What a waste of time."

"No, it wasn't. You got to ask your questions and meet people who knew him, loved him."

"Thanks for your help," I said, though I couldn't meet his eyes. "And for..." I glanced around the flat, flushed and coughed. "Yeah...for everything."

"You should take me with you."

I blinked. "What?"

"Take me with you. To meet Novák."

"Why?"

"I've tried to get a meeting with Ivor Novák for years but never even got close. But if you take me, I know he'll see me."

"What do you want with him?"

"I can help," he said, coming around the sofa. "And not just with the book. With everything I know, with my contacts in the human world, I could really make a difference if he made me part of his campaign."

"He's not my friend," I said patiently. "He's some alien overlord that has interfered with my life and tried to play god."

Jay pursed his lips. "This is important to me. I want to be part of it."

I glanced at his neck, now hidden behind the collar of his top, then glanced away. "It's not up to me."

"Alec—"

"Jay, please," I said, putting my hand on the door handle. "Thank you for your help...really. But I'm going to talk to Novák, pass on what Ana Bonny said, then I'm going home. That's it."

His face fell. "That's it?"

I sighed. "You know what I mean."

He nodded stiffly, managing a ghost of his former smile. "I think I do."

Chapter Seven

I got a taxi out to Hampstead to collect my car then drove back to the hotel. The musky smell of Jay's hair and skin was still on my clothing. I pulled on a clean shirt, attempted to yank my unruly hair into some semblance of order, gave up then hurried out of the building. I drove through the choked London traffic to Novák's building with my mind racing. My skin still felt warm where Jay had touched it.

I found the entrance to the underground garage on my second circuit of the building and was just scanning for a buzzer when the door began to rumble open on its own. I frowned at the camera over the door then drove inside. The lift was open and waiting, and all too soon I was stepping again into Novák's apartment.

"Lord Aviemore," he said, raising from his seat with liquid grace and moving to the drinks counter. "Good to see you. I hope you are quite recovered from your little ordeal?"

I gave him a look. "Which one?"

"The little forced afternoon tea with the Brassingtons."

"Terje told you. He got my message."

"He did," he surveyed me a moment. "I don't doubt for a moment you were able to handle yourself, but please assure me they didn't harm you? Or threaten you in any way?"

"Harm me? No. Threaten me?" I shrugged. "Not overtly, no. But Terje told you what they said?"

"He did."

"Not good."

"Not on the face of it," he said. "But they've shown their hand now. This is to our advantage."

"I'm pleased for you," I said flatly.

I got the distinct impression that if it hadn't been for centuries-honed patience, he would have sighed. Instead, he just lifted his thick, black eyebrows a fraction. "And how did it go at Forest Hill?"

"Not great," I muttered. "Where's Terje?"

"Not here," Novák said, holding out another glass of whiskey. "I think his assignment will keep him away for some days, especially with what happened yesterday. If we find out how they know about Terje, we may discover more of what they're planning. As for your assignment, I'm impressed you were allowed entry to Forest Hill so quickly."

"I...had help."

"Ah, yes," Novák said, pouring a whiskey for himself. "This would be the young Mr. Singh?"

I blinked. "You had me followed?"

"No," Novák said, turning on the TV with his remote. "*He* followed *you*."

The camera feed showed Jay hovering outside the garage, searching for a way to get in. I swore.

"I know Mr. Singh by reputation. He's one of our valued human allies. He has done much for us. Though, because of his connection to you, I have considered it unwise to involve him too directly, in case he stumbled onto the truth."

"I knew him a long time ago," I said carefully.

Novák weighed me up a long moment then sipped his drink. "If you think we can trust him, I would like to have him on board." I stared out of the window. "Well? Can we trust him?"

"He's passionate about haemophile rights," I said. "I think he was in love with one, once. Doing his part seems to mean a lot to him."

"And you would be comfortable with that?"

"Why wouldn't I be?" He looked at me heavily. I scowled. "What? Can you smell him on me or something?"

"Yes."

"Jesus Christ…"

"I don't mean to offend," he said, looking thoughtfully at the screen, where Jay was moving from one camera feed to another, still looking for a way in. "The intricacies of human relationships are lost on me, I'm afraid. But I'm aware enough to know to ask."

"Involve him or don't," I said, drinking the whiskey, "I don't really care. I've done what you've asked. I just want to go home."

"Very well." He pushed a button on the drinks counter. "Collinson? There is a young gentleman attempting to gain entry at the North Gate. Show him in, would you?"

"Now?" I grated.

"Why not?"

"I told you that I'm done. I want to get out of here."

117

"I'm not stopping you, my lord."

I made an impatient noise. "I'm not leaving without Terje."

"Like I said, I don't expect him to be done for some days yet. I can provide you with accommodations if you wish to wait. But the safest thing for you to do would be to return to Glenroe and wait for him there."

I was about to reply when the lift doors slid open and out stepped Collinson, followed closely by Jay.

"Mr. Jason Singh," she announced, then withdrew. Jay looked around him. His gaze landed on Novák and his eyes widened.

"Mr. Singh," Novák said, "good of you to join us. May I offer you some refreshment?"

"Rådgiver Novák," Jay said, glancing nervously at me and coming forward, holding out his hand. "It is a great pleasure to meet you, sir."

"And you, Mr. Singh," Novák said, taking Jay's hand. He held out a tumbler of whiskey with the other, which Jay accepted. "I know you by reputation, of course. And our mutual friend Lord Aviemore has informed me of your interest in working with me."

"That's right, sir," Jay said. "The only way to make progress is to alter human perceptions. I'm planning a series of articles ahead of the release of my book, which I hope, with your endorsement, will —"

He cut off as the lift doors slid open again and out stepped Terje. He froze, stiller than stone, just inside the room. His silver eyes, glinting like moonlit ice, slid from me to Jay and I knew he knew. The bottom dropped out of my stomach.

"Terje," Novák said, putting down his glass, the faintest line appearing between his eyebrows. "I wasn't expecting you."

Terje didn't speak. I couldn't. Jay stared at him, his face pale.

"Terje... Terje Kristiansen?" Jay's gaze shifted from my lover to me, hardening as it did so. "Alec? What's going on?"

My mind clamored but my mouth didn't open.

"This is...unfortunate," Novák said.

"He's supposed to be dead," Jay said, his voice hard.

"He did die," I said. "Ogdell shot him with an automatic rifle. He bled to death, in agony..." Jay's face creased, and I stepped closer, lowering my voice. "Jon Ogdell murdered him. In cold blood. Out of hate. That all happened. It's just that he...came back."

"Came back?"

"They're different," I said, looking to Novák and Terje for help, but they just watched us in silence. "Sometimes they can...come back. The Blood brings them back."

"So why lie?" Jay asked.

"It was necessary," Novák said, "for the greater good."

"I can't believe this." Jay shook his head, staring at Novák. "This is... This is an abuse of trust. People have faith in you. They're relying on you to fight for their cause and you've lied about this, one of the most influential events—"

"I understand the implications," Novák said, holding Jay's accusing gaze without reaction. "But both to further our cause and for Terje's own safety, I judged it the best course of action."

Jay looked at me. "And you, Alec? Why'd *you* lie?" I downed my whiskey and didn't meet any of the eyes on me. After a pained moment, Jay turned back to

Novák. "Rådgiver Novák... All due respect, but I believe this was a serious misjudgment."

"You must understand, Mr. Singh," Novák replied, "that I see more than you do. And the wellbeing of my people is, and will always be, my first priority."

No one spoke for some time. I looked around, feeling the deep, black voids dividing us all.

"Terje," Novák finally broke the silence, "do you have something to report?"

"Yes," Terje said without intonation.

"Go ahead," Novák ordered. "I think we're all still allies here?"

Jay's face was tight. Terje's gaze stayed on me but I couldn't penetrate the steel curtain behind his eyes. He looked away and turned to Novák.

"After Alec's message, I followed his scent and found the underground stronghold the Brassingtons have been using to hold meetings," he spoke levelly, without intonation, but Jay gaped at me and I winced. "They held a gathering there last night with a number of their associates. There were haemophiles present."

"Haemophiles?" Jay started. "Meeting with the Brassingtons?"

Terje's cut-glass gaze appraised Jay, but Novák spoke before he could say anything, "As I feared. Go on, Terje."

"The haemophiles have been given civilian targets to kill, with instructions to leave the bodies in conspicuous places."

"What?" Jay paled. "Why?"

Terje's icy gaze landed on him. "They plan to stir mistrust and fear and, off the back of that, announce their intention to run in the next election with a campaign to tighten haemophile restrictions."

Jay's face flushed. Novák's didn't change. "Did they mention the intended victims' names? Or dates?"

"Some," Terje said, holding out an envelope.

Novák took it. "Thank you, Terje. Hopefully we can stop this tide before it starts to turn."

"That information needs to go to the authorities," Jay started.

"It will be taken care of," Novák said, tucking the envelope inside his jacket. "Terje, Lord Aviemore, thank you for all your assistance." He glanced between our awkward gathering with a very human awareness in his eyes. "I advise you to return to Glenroe. I will be in touch if anything further comes to light that you should be aware of."

Terje nodded and strode to the lift. I hurried after him but Jay called my name.

I hesitated, and in that moment, the doors of the lift slid closed between me and Terje. Jay stepped to my side.

"You could have told me," he said in a pained whisper.

"I couldn't," I replied, intensely aware of Novák watching.

"You *could*," Jay insisted.

"We all agreed to keep it secret," I replied. "Novák had a campaign to build. Terje and I wanted to be left alone. And if that ex-Magister of his finds out he's still alive—"

"That's *not* why you didn't tell me."

Heat rushed into my face. "Look, Jay—"

"Everything you said," he said bitterly, "and everything you didn't say… Alec, can't you see how twisted this is? Even forgetting the fact that we fucked—"

"Jay—"

"You *lied* to me. To everyone. Why?"

"I had to."

"No, you *wanted* to. But for what? You're in so much pain, Alec. I thought it was because you were grieving…" He gripped my arm. "Why? If he's still here, why do you feel that way?"

I pulled my arm out of his grip and summoned the lift. He said my name again, but I stepped in without replying. The doors closed, hiding his pained look from my view.

Terje was in the driver's seat of the Jaguar with the engine running when I reached the garage. I climbed in with my stomach tying itself in knots.

"Terje…"

"It's okay," Terje said, pulling out of the space and steering toward the doors.

I frowned. "Don't you think we should talk about this?"

"About what?"

"About Jay."

The garage door rumbled open. Terje pulled out into the streaming traffic. I shifted in my seat. "Terje—"

"It's all right," he cut me off, his gaze fixed ahead. "You don't have to explain anything."

Heat surged through my chest. "You can't seriously—"

"Alec," he said, finally looking at me, though his face was blank, "you're overreacting. You had sex. It's healthy. Natural. I understand."

"I don't want you to just *understand*."

Terje frowned, pulling out into a faster lane. "Then what do you want?"

"I want you to be angry," I said, my voice shaking. "I cheated on you. I..." I made a frustrated noise and ran a hand over my face. "Christ. I fucked someone else, Terje. Don't you care?"

Terje raised his eyebrows. "He was human. You had a connection...and a need. Why should I care?"

"Because I want to *mean* something to you."

"You do."

"So haemophiles really don't care about fidelity? Trust?"

"Look, Alec," he said, the start of an exasperated smile on his smooth, pale lips. "Fidelity is one thing. Monogamy is another. Sex is different for your kind. You already know that. This hasn't changed how I feel about you — or me wanting to have that experience with you again. I just think what you and I have..." He shrugged again. "It's more than that, isn't it?"

I stared at him, then out of the window. "If you really don't care, then what was all that before?"

"All what?"

"When you first came in the room. When you saw Jay. When you...smelled him, smelled what we'd done. You felt something. I know you did. You looked like you were about to bite his head off. Literally."

He was silent for a long, considered moment, his face blank. "I suppose I was just...surprised."

"Surprised?"

"After what you'd said to me in Edinburgh," he spoke, slowly, carefully, like he was weighing out each word, "I thought perhaps faithfulness of this sort was important to you. You often surprise me, Alec." His voice had levelled out, "I suppose I just didn't expect to be surprised in that way."

"That was your reaction? Surprise?"

He drove for a time without looking at me. "I take it that's not enough?"

I couldn't find a way to reply.

It was a long, uncomfortable drive back to Glenroe, at least for me. I dozed some of the way but then just dreamed about arguing further. I would wake more frustrated and more guilty each time.

Terje didn't appear to notice.

By the time I was bolting the front door of Glenroe behind us, I was aching, exhausted and sullen. Dawn wasn't far off and Terje had already disappeared. I dumped my bag on the floor of the master bedroom and sat on the bed to pull off my shoes. I stared around at the room I'd loved so much when I'd left it. Now it felt empty...hollow.

I collapsed onto the bed with a weariness that went right to my bones.

Terje brushing his hand up my leg made me jump. I sat up. He was perched on the edge of the bed, his shirt and shoes gone, his hair loose on his shoulders and his cool, pale skin slightly warmed by a recent feed. He ran his hand along my thigh. My flesh tingled and my breath caught in my chest.

I opened my mouth to speak but he climbed on top of me and stopped me with a firm, hungry kiss. I whimpered, immediately hard, even as cold waves of guilt and thoughts of Jay threatened to douse my arousal.

As if guessing my thoughts, Terje pulled at my clothing, steadily, patiently unbuttoning and unzipping, stripping each layer away with slow, deliberate care. The snowmelt silver of his eyes glinted in the low light from the bedside lamp.

"You really want to? After what I've done?"

"You know I won't give you the right answer," Terje said softly into my ear, "so don't even ask."

A confused tangle of emotions rolled through my insides, but then Terje's familiar weight rested across my legs and he was bending and taking my hard, aching cock into his mouth.

I gasped. Lightning flickered along my nerves. He gripped my thighs. I panted his name, crushed my eyes shut and all the guilt, hurt and confusion were swept away like a sandcastle in the rising tide. He worked me slowly, up and down, languid, sensuous movements that drove me mad even as they teased me with waves of pleasure. He brought me so close that the muscles in my abdomen and legs bunched in anticipation, then he pulled away.

The sudden chill made me shiver. He laid his weight along me, kissing me deeply. He'd shed his jeans and the hard length of his erection pressed against my thigh. I kissed him back and reached for him, but he took hold of my wrist and pinned it above my head. He lifted his head to peer into my face. He gazed at me from the dark, unknowable depths of his eyes and I felt like I would drown in them.

"I think it's important I show you how I feel," he whispered, sliding a hand down my body and lifting my knee. "As I seem unable to phrase it in words in a way that satisfies you." He ran his hand between us, between my legs. He didn't break eye contact as the pads of his fingers swept over my entrance. I quivered.

"Terje…"

He ran his tongue up my neck as he massaged the tight opening. My pulse thundered in my throat and my groin.

"Let me show you, Alec," he whispered in my ear. "Let me show you how you make me feel."

I nodded stiffly, unable to speak. I felt him smile against my neck, then he was reaching into the bedside table drawer. He withdrew the lube I kept in there for my own use. I blushed, inexplicably embarrassed by the fact that he knew where I kept it, and saw in the answering twitch of his lips that he knew what I was thinking.

"It's best you prepare yourself," he said softly, lifting my hand and squeezing some of the cool, slick liquid into it.

"You won't hurt me," I whispered.

He ran his sharp fingernails through my stubble with a smile that was a little sad. "I'm afraid I would. And besides…maybe I want to watch."

I shuddered with pleasure. He sat beside me, his gaze intent, one hand working his own erection almost lazily. I locked my eyes with his, smeared the lube on my fingers and reached between my legs. I shivered as I pressed against the tight ring of muscle, clenching my eyes shut. I breathed through the discomfort and slid in a finger. Sparks lit inside my gut and I lay still, waiting until the feeling of invasion subsided.

"Have you done it this way before?" he asked, brushing kisses along my shoulder.

I nodded, my eyes still shut as I worked my finger farther in, searching, reaching. It brushed against that spot deep inside that ignited my nerves, and all my muscles clenched. "Yes," I forced out, "once."

"You prefer it the other way."

"Yeah," I said, forcing my eyes open and meeting his, "but I want to know you this way."

He ran his hand along my arm then cupped the hand with the finger buried inside me. He guided a second finger inside without breaking eye contact. I gritted my teeth and breathed deep, making myself relax. He tightened his grip on my hand and started to move it, pushing my fingers deeper.

"I want to make you feel this," he murmured as he sucked at my earlobe. "Help you feel a little of what I feel when you fuck me. How good it is." I groaned as my fingers swept over the sensitive spot, and soon my cock was weeping and trembling.

"Terje," I warned, then found he was holding a finger to my lips. The heady, fruit-thick smell of Blood filled my head. I trembled with the onslaught of sensations. I wanted to refuse it—to prove I could, that I wanted to feel him naturally, as a human. But when I knew I was seconds from coming, I took the finger into my mouth.

The flavor and scent ballooned through me, slowing everything down, even as it heightened every sensation. I could still feel my fingers stretching, sweeping, plumbing my very depths, as well as the pressure of the orgasm building at the base of my cock, but I was no longer in danger of being swept away. Now I was immersed, surrounded, like I was sinking into the darkest depths of a sun-warmed lake. Despite the dampening effect of the Blood, knowing that this was how Terje felt when I fucked him with my fingers almost undid me.

He moaned, like he knew, and seized my mouth in a deep, possessive kiss. Thrusting my digits in with one hand, I began to pump my cock with the other.

"Fuck, Terje..." I spoke as if from a great distance. "Christ...I can't... I don't know how much of this I can take."

"Let's find out," he muttered against my lips, releasing his hold and taking a firm grip of my hips instead. "Turn over."

I hurried to obey, every inch of me thrumming in anticipation. "You've done it this way before?"

"I've done it pretty much every way possible in my time," he said with the softness of a smile in his voice. "Some ways that aren't even considered possible."

"With humans?"

"We're not thinking about anyone else right now," he said, running his hands over my back and arse. I shivered then heard the cap of the lubricant bottle again, and the mattress shifting as he knelt between my legs. He leaned over me, brushing feathery kisses across my neck and into my hair.

"Are you ready?"

I nodded against the pillow, clenching my eyes shut. Then his slick hardness was pressing against my entrance. I hissed in a breath between clenched teeth. He felt a lot bigger than I expected, partly because I was so unused to bottoming but also because I'd never known him in this way. I held my breath as he slid in, filling and stretching me in a way that generated a potent mix of pleasure and pain. I shifted, getting onto my elbows and knees. He moved with me, pushing deeper. I moaned, the intensity almost too much. He was murmuring into my hair, but I couldn't make sense of the words.

He withdrew slowly. The loss of pressure made me shake, then he was sliding in again. He pushed until he was seated all the way, pressing his hips against my arse. His hardness brushed the place inside me that made spots dance in my vision, and I let out a strangled noise. I angled myself to take him farther, moaning into the pillow as his cock rubbed against my prostate again.

"*Gud*, Alec," he panted into my hair.

"Move," I said, "please."

He straightened, took a firmer grip of my hips, pulled out, then thrust back in, faster this time. I cried a word close to his name, then he repeated the motion, harder…and again.

I lost the ability to form words as he increased his pace. He pushed my legs wider with his knee and leaned over me, the powerful muscles in his thighs bunching as he deepened the angle. My own limbs weakened, and I fought to stay on my elbows. As if sensing this, he looped an arm under my chest. He held me close and pounded into me, his breath brushing my ear, moaning deep and low in his chest in a way I hadn't heard before.

When he reached around to start working my cock, I could no longer hear anything. I was drowning in pleasure, suffocating in it. It was only his inhuman strength that kept me from collapsing. The impending orgasm rumbled like a volcano behind my ribs. I dug my fingers into the sheets and bit my lip so hard that I tasted blood.

I came in waves, like a forest fire leaping a firebreak, as if a cardiac arrest were seizing my body and sweeping my soul away. My hot seed spattered against my belly and legs, and my limbs finally gave out.

He thrust once more and held himself there, his body shaking as he cried out my name.

I lay on my side with him curled against my back until the world stopped spinning. My flesh slowly cooled as my pulse returned to normal, human levels. His breaths were calm and steady against my neck, and his long limbs were twined with mine. He'd pulled out, but I could still feel the stretch, smoldering like the last embers of a bonfire.

"It's getting light," I whispered, seeing dawn starting to silver the edges of the blinds.

"I know."

I turned to face him. The flush had already faded from his cheeks. If it weren't for his tousled hair and nakedness, no one would be able to tell that anything had happened. I put aside that troubled thought and reached out to brush the strands of hair out of his face.

"Thank you," I said.

"For what?"

"For understanding that sometimes I need to understand, even when I can't."

He pressed a gentle kiss to my lips. "I try, Alec. I do try."

"I know," I said, reaching for his hand and holding it tight. "Perhaps I could try harder."

He sighed. "We can't always be trying — fighting everything, fighting each other. Just feel what you need to feel. That's all I do. It's all I'm capable of."

"But you don't seem to feel anything." I hadn't meant to say it, but my defenses were in tatters and it just fell out of me.

"I feel, Alec. You know I feel."

"Then why — ?"

"I care that you slept with that boy." He cut me off. "But only because it's the first sign of you realizing that I can't give you everything you need."

"That's not true."

"It is," he said softly. "For now—for some years, I hope—that need will just be a physical thing. That's why I don't care in the way you want me to about you 'cheating'." I opened my mouth to protest, but he spoke over me. "Alec, that side of things doesn't affect me the way it affects you. You know fidelity in the way you mean it is just an animal instinct to protect your bloodline?"

I snorted. "I'm not likely to reproduce with Jay…or anyone."

"Your biology doesn't know that," he said, brushing the sweaty strands of hair behind my ears. "But mine knows sex has nothing to do with reproduction, so we feel differently about it. That's all."

"It would hurt me if you slept with someone else, biology or not."

"I know it would," he said gently, "which is why I wouldn't. I don't want to, anyway." His smile was a little weary. "You're the only one who makes me want to feel these things. No one else has for a long time."

I stared up into the bed curtains, some of the tension easing from my limbs.

"I met Ana Bonny at Forest Hill," I murmured. He didn't say anything. I rolled my head on the pillow. He was contemplating me with an unreadable expression. "She said you and she were…close."

"We were," he said softly, "for a long time. But that's different."

"And the human lover?" I asked. "The one you had before me? The one who got you into trouble?"

"What about him?"

Him. I swallowed, then took a moment to get on top of my reaction. "Did you love him?"

"No."

I went very still, like a spell would break if I moved. "Was it Jay?" I asked in almost a whisper.

Terje looked confused. "The boy you were with last night?"

I winced. "He had a haemophile lover once. It…didn't work out. And he seems pretty messed up by it."

"So why would you think that was me?"

"I don't know," I said and rubbed my eyes, suddenly exhausted. "I know I'm jealous, Terje. I guess I just want to know who to be jealous of."

He laughed. "Sometimes I'm glad I'm not human anymore," he said, his soft smile taking any sting out of his words. "The emotions are so complicated. No. It wasn't Jay Singh. Besides" — he frowned — "whoever he was with drank from him for pleasure. I could tell just by looking at him. I would never do that."

I nodded, reassured and unsettled in equal measure.

"Don't overthink it, Alec," he said pressing another kiss to my cheek. "We are what we are, and that's more than enough for now."

The bed dipped as he left it and scooped his jeans from the floor.

"For how long?"

"Until it's not."

He left, clicking the door shut behind him. I lay in the cool sheets, staring at the ceiling. Dawn was breaking outside. I was exhausted, emotionally and physically. There were pin-point cuts around my hips where his fingernails had broken the skin. My arse still burned. The sheets were damp, sticky and smelled like sex. It had been good. I felt like I knew him again, that I belonged to him and he to me. But his words, his hesitancy, the void between us that even an amazing fuck couldn't bridge, still weighed heavy in my chest.

I turned onto my side, telling myself it would be different after I'd slept. Then I saw the missed call and text message notifications on my phone from Jay.

Alec, I'm sorry for what I said. I think we should talk. Please call x

I stared at the kiss at the end of the message for a long time before switching my phone off, drawing up the covers and closing my eyes.

Chapter Eight

I woke about an hour before sunset with a stiff neck and a sore arse. Despite everything, the unfamiliar burn made me smile. I listened until I heard the last of the construction crew driving away, then showered, wincing as the hot water washed over the cuts on my hips. I dressed, choosing one of my smarter shirts and my newest jeans, and hurried downstairs, thinking to eat before Terje woke. Then I'd suggest a walk — a long one, all night maybe, like the ones we'd had done when he first moved in. We could find a spot high in the mountains to sit, drink wine and watch the stars move across the sky.

I reheated some leftovers then packed a bottle of wine and some picnic glasses into a backpack. I pulled on my walking boots and sat in the drawing room to wait.

Terje appeared at my elbow a few minutes after sunset. He smiled at me a little regretfully as I stood and hoisted the backpack onto my shoulders.

"I thought we could —"

"I've had a call from Novák," he said. "The information you got at Forest Hill... I have to follow up on it."

"I didn't get any information."

"The fact that she bypassed her commune implies she's planning something she doesn't want them involved in," he said. "Novák's worried it might be tied in with the Brassingtons' plans. He's setting things in motion to apprehend their haemophile associates before anything happens, but there are a few things I need to check myself."

"No," I said, slamming the bag onto a table. "We've done more than enough."

"Alec..."

"I'm not having this fight again, Terje."

"Then don't." His eyes were cool. My insides felt like they were about to burst. Finally, he sighed and turned away. "You can still walk if you want to. You'll be safe. Just don't go too far."

He left without looking back.

I stood in the drawing room, the cold and hollowness returning, before cursing, shouldering the bag and heading outside.

The cool mountain air soothed the burning under my skin and was fresh in my lungs. The physical toll of the climb went some way to relieving the pressure that had built in my head. Soon I could no longer see the lights from Glenroe. I took a sheep track that wound around the mountain and down toward the next glen. There I found a level spot among some boulders where I dropped to the scrubby grass and pulled out the wine. I drank while glowering into the moonlit glen, wondering at how cold and remote the place now seemed.

It was as I swallowed the last mouthful that I realized I wasn't alone.

I started, scrambled to my feet and turned on my torch. A haemophile stood beside one of the boulders, stiller than the ancient stone. She didn't blink when the bright light shone into her eyes. She stood with her hands in the pockets of a light walking coat, watching me. Her skin was a luscious, dark brown, made richer by the preternatural haemophile luster that almost made it glow, like a candle behind tinted glass. Her eyes were blacker than the night sky overhead. Her thick, black hair was braided against her scalp. The smooth curve her of forehead was unlined, but she didn't look young. Her eyes were too deep, her face too knowing.

I swallowed the wine trying to climb back up my throat. "Who are you?"

"Hati Nenge, Lord Aviemore," she lilted in a strong East African accent. When nothing else was forthcoming, I blinked at her.

"What do you want?"

She blinked this time, her long black lashes sweeping down and up again. "From you? Nothing."

I gripped the torch tighter. "Then why are you here?"

"Rådgiver Novák said I should make myself known to you," she said, each word weighted and slow, like she didn't speak out loud often.

"Why?"

"I've guarded Glenroe for some time, but Novák has now told me that perhaps you would be *happier*" — she made the word sound like a sneer — "meeting me in person."

I attempted to get my muddled thoughts in line. "Guarded?"

"Yes. Your estate. The land around it."

"Against what?"

"Anyone intent on harm."

I went cold. "Has there been anyone?"

"A few."

I blanched. "Human?"

"No."

My head started to spin. "Who were they?"

"I don't know."

I glared. "What do you mean you don't know?"

"It's not my job to know."

"Did the Brassingtons send them?"

"I don't know."

"But you kept them away?"

"Yes." She narrowed her eyes slightly. "It unsettles you, but it is necessary."

I rubbed my temples to ease a growing ache. "It was you...in the caves?"

"That's where I sleep. I did not expect to be disturbed there."

"Well, if I'd known..."

"Telling you wasn't considered necessary."

"And Terje? Does he know?"

"Possibly. It's not easy for us to hide from each other. Though he himself...takes something." She frowned. "It makes him harder to detect."

I swallowed a sour aftertaste. "Someone's trying to kill me?"

"Or Kristiansen," she shrugged. "Or both of you. I really don't know, my lord. I just follow my orders."

I scowled at her. "Do you people ever get fed up with being this way?"

"What way?"

"Not feeling. Not caring. Not thinking for yourself."

"We do all those things," she said levelly, "just not the same way you do."

"So spending weeks wandering the mountains alone, sleeping in a cave, guarding two people you don't know for reasons you don't know or don't care about... You think that's normal?"

She examined him blankly for a long moment. "Why do you care what I think?"

"I just want to *understand.*"

"Yes, they've said that about you," she said contemplatively. She sighed and gestured along the path. "We should walk and talk, I think."

"Why?"

"You're drunk. It's getting cold. And there's someone at the house."

I started. "Who?"

"Someone new...not a threat."

I gathered myself with an effort, shouldered my bag and started off down the path.

"To answer your question," she murmured as she fell into step beside me, "yes, it is normal. Obeying your Magister is normal."

"Novák is your Magister?"

She lifted one shoulder. "More or less. I'm a Registered Independent. No commune. But I've known Novák a long time."

"So, you don't have a commune, but you still come running when he calls?"

"Yes."

"Why?"

She gave him a sideways glance. "There is a very particular sort of freedom in putting your trust in forces greater than yourself."

"Novák is a force greater than you?"

"Novák. Any Magister." She looked at him again then away. "They're older. Wiser. More powerful. You do what they ask, and they look out for you. That's what a commune is."

"But you choose not to have one?"

"Registered Independent means living outside a traditional, settled commune. It doesn't mean you're alone. You can never be alone."

"Or free."

"That depends on your perception."

"Sounds like being trapped to me."

"You humans have your gods. Your governments. We have each other."

"You think of your Magisters as gods?"

"Not as you mean the word, but it's the only comparison. We have nothing else."

I glared at the path. "I don't believe in any god…or government, either."

"Then you are unusual."

"Hardly."

Nenge walked without looking where she was going, almost floating over the uneven ground, and she spoke dreamily, like her mind was elsewhere. "There are plenty of humans who don't believe in any church-taught god, it's true, and plenty more who think their government is shambolic, corrupt or incompetent. But they all still *believe* — believe that one, or the other or both are *doing* something. Taking care of things, even if they don't always do it well."

"Beliefs like that just allow other people to mess with your life."

"But what's the alternative?" she asked with a sideways glance. "I'll tell you, Lord Aviemore. Anarchy. I've seen it among both our kinds. No one comes out of that well."

"So blind loyalty is the lesser of two evils?"

"Much lesser." I frowned, something cold ghosting under my belly at her tone. "Those of us without links?" she went on. "The exiled? The outcasts? They're where monster legends come from. And the legends don't come close."

I scuffed the ground with my foot. "I don't care about evil, or politics, or the best way to run the world. I...*we* just want to be left out of it."

She was silent for a time. When she spoke again, her voice was lower. "I don't know Terje Kristiansen, but as he's one of us, I can tell you that's not what he wants. He wouldn't forsake everything he knows, everything he is."

"He has me," I insisted.

"Yes, and one day you'll be dead. Then where will he be?"

I stopped walking. She stopped just inside the light from my torch. A dark chasm opened in the back of my mind. "I..." My voice cracked. I swallowed, tried again. "I don't know. I hadn't thought that far ahead. He could find another..."

"If he's left a commune to be with you, it's because you're different. He won't find another like you. But whether you're worth sacrificing his future for or not remains the question."

"Why are you saying these things?"

"You asked."

I swiped at the wetness beading in the corners of my eyes.

She made a noise that was close to a sigh. "You've been in the cavern that lies to the south of your home, yes? Your scent is faint, old, but it is there."

"The Ballroom?" I asked blearily.

"A beautiful name," she said in a low, dreamy voice. "Yes, the Ballroom. A wonderful place."

"What has that to do with anything?"

"I am trying to explain. You understand this place, the Ballroom, yes? It is part of the world, shaped by it—untold years old, amazing to see, and yet it exists in the dark, outside of awareness." She gazed at me with her heavy gaze. "This is like us. We were here before you were born. We will be here long after you're gone. We may spend some time in each other's company…but in the end, the only thing that shapes us is a slow drip of water, changes too slow for a human to see. You can't expect us to change quicker, just for you."

"Someone told me…" I started, choked. I cleared my throat and started again. "Another haemophile told me it's possible. That we can be happy together…if we want to be."

She shrugged. "Possible, yes. For your lifetime at least. But for him?" She shrugged again. "You're asking a lot." She gestured down the path and, with a tremendous effort, I managed to make my feet move.

We reached the ridge. The lights of Glenroe punched holes in the night below. An unfamiliar car was pulled up in the garage forecourt and a lone, slim figure was wandering along the line of finished restoration projects. My belly flopped. I turned to say something more to Nenge, but she had vanished. I took a couple of deep lungfuls of the cool night air and picked my way down to the house.

"Jay?"

He straightened from his examination of the Triumph Herald with a smile. The expression slipped as he took in the look on my face.

"Hey, Alec," he said. "I tried calling…"

"I don't get reception."

"None at all?" I frowned at the floor. "I've come a long way," he continued. "You could at least talk to me."

"I'm sorry about the other night," I mumbled. "I shouldn't have let it happen."

"I don't need you to be sorry," he said. "I just need you to explain."

"Explain what?"

He paused. "Is he here?"

"No."

"Then can we go in?"

He followed me inside and stopped in the hall, gawking at the grand staircase, the chandelier, the paintings on the walls.

"Wow," he breathed as we moved through to the drawing room. "This place is incredible…"

"We've done a lot."

"He paid for all this?"

I winced, pouring whiskey into tumblers on the sideboard. "Most of it."

Jay gazed around at the polished wood, gleaming silverware and the deep sofas and chairs that surrounded the marble fireplace. His gaze landed on the dark, moody landscape painting over the mantle.

"Jacob More?"

"Yes."

"An original?"

"Yes."

Jay accepted the drink I held out to him without taking his eyes from the painting. "I wouldn't have thought it would be your style."

"It was Dad's," I said, swallowing a large mouthful. "The only thing of his I kept. Helps me remember."

"Remember what?"

I regarded the dark colors, the twisted trees, the white water spilling over the rushing waterfall, the crumbling ruins in the background. "The world goes on."

"Is that right?" He was next to me, his gaze no longer on the painting.

"What did you want, Jay?"

"To talk."

"I don't know what you want me to say."

His eyes were bright with a very human pain. "What happened, Alec? Between us?"

I gritted my teeth. "I said I'm sorry…"

"Again," he said, drawing me to sit on the couch, "I don't want you to be sorry. I'm not sorry. What we did…" Color rushed into his cheeks. "It was good. I've not…" He let out a nervous laugh. "Let's just say it's been a while since it's been that good for me. And you, well…" He lowered his voice. "It felt like you enjoyed it too. Needed it, even."

"Jay—"

"I'm happy for you, Alec," he said, "that you have each other, after everything you went through."

"That's not what you said to Novák."

"What he did was wrong. But I *think* I can understand your reasons for keeping things secret…to

143

build a life." His expression grew troubled. "So why are you still hurting?"

"I'm not."

He gave me a sardonic look. "Alec..."

"You've misunderstood," I insisted, fighting the blur of the alcohol that threatened to bring down the walls holding my temper in check. "What I did with you...it was a mistake, a moment of weakness. I..." I made an impatient noise, searching for words. "I got caught in the moment."

"You don't believe that—not really."

"What do you *want*, Jay?"

"Come on, Alec. You're not that unused to reading people."

"You'd be surprised."

He shifted closer. "I want *you*, Alec...to be with you."

"I'm spoken for."

His jaw worked. "Whatever this is, it's hurting you. *He's* hurting you."

"Stop."

"We can't be with them," Jay went on, setting his untasted glass on the coffee table. "Not for long." His voice was strained, his gaze intent. "He'll destroy you."

"Look... I don't know what your experience was like—"

"He almost killed me," Jay said, curling his hand into a fist. "And not from feeding on me, before you say it." His skin had paled but for high spots of color on each cheek. His eyes were dark and feverish. "He made me feel more than I'd ever felt before. Made me aware of a kind of existence, of a depth of feeling I'd never dreamed was possible. Then, one day, he was gone. No word, no explanation just...gone." He took a shaking breath, his eyes going right through me like he could no longer see me. "I was…in a bad place. For a long time. I didn't think I'd ever come back from that edge. The only reason I did was because I realized he couldn't *help* but hurt me. It's just their nature." He took a shaking breath and clasped his hands in his lap. "That was when I knew I had to help change the way we think about them…before we all destroy each other."

"Terje and I—"

"I understand," he insisted, brushing the hair back from my face. "I do, Alec. You think it's forever. It's not." His mouth was so close, so expressive, wounded, soft-looking. I remembered the taste of him, the way he moved, how hot our skin became when we moved together. I shut my eyes.

"I'm sorry, Jay."

He wrapped his hand around mine and held on tight. "Let me help you, Alec. Let me take you away from all this."

"This is my home."

"Then send him away…"

"I love him." My breath caught as I realized what I'd said.

Jay looked shocked, but then he shook his head sadly. "You don't, Alec. You don't even know him."

"*You* don't know him."

"Don't do this to yourself. Besides everything else, think of this political mess that's going on. It's only going to get worse. If you're with him, you'll be caught in the middle of it all…again."

"I can't leave him. I don't *want* to leave him."

"He's dangerous."

"He would never let anything hurt me."

"Even if that's true," Jay went on, squeezing my hand tighter, "even if he protects you from the political fallout and Evgeniya is caught and you're able to just be together, even if you get everything you want...eventually, he will ruin you, Alec."

"He cares about me."

"For now."

I pulled myself from his grip and stood with my back to him, my body shaking. "I'd like you to leave now."

"Well, I'm not going to," he said, stepping close behind me. "You're drunk. You're alone. You're in pain."

"What else is new?"

He turned me to face him with a firm grip on my shoulders. He looked deep into my eyes. "I care about you, Alec, have for a long time. And take it from someone who knows... Terje may not plan to hurt you, but he will." His eyes were bright. "It's impossible not to be sucked right in. And, for a while, they can feel the same way. But we're too different, Alec."

"I thought you were pro-haemo?"

"I am. Part of my work is to educate people, to help humans understand so we can live together in peace. But some of what I know I've learned the hard way. I want to spare others that. Spare you."

"You can't know what will happen to us."

"Does he love you?"

"He could," I snapped. "He might...one day."

Jay snaked an arm around my waist and pressed his face into my shoulder. He let out a shuddering breath against my skin. "He won't, Alec. He can't."

I pulled out of the embrace. "Leave, Jay. *Now*."

"Please listen."

"I've heard enough."

"You've not listened to anything I've said."

"You've gotten what you want," I said. "You're in with Novák. Go on your little crusade. Maybe he'll ask to suck on your neck. Who knows?"

"That's not fair."

"*Leave.*"

His face hardened. "You're making a mistake."

"*Out.*"

He slammed the door as he left. The noise echoed around the silent, empty house. I flung my tumbler at the fireplace. It shattered, bright shards scattering across the hearth. I collapsed onto the sofa, my head in my hands.

I waited there all night, praying Terje would return and help push everything Jay and Nenge had said out of my head.

He didn't.

Chapter Nine

I woke, groggy and with a foul taste in my mouth, to the clunking sound of metal clashing on metal and grumbling voices. Sunlight poured through the drawing room windows, knifing into my skull. I groaned and unwound myself from the couch, wincing at the sight of the broken glass in the grate and the empty whiskey decanter on its side on the rug.

I rubbed my head and went to the window. I frowned at the workmen loading the scaffolding onto a truck.

I pushed my hair into some sort of order, retrieved a pair of sunglasses, pushed my feet into the walking boots I'd left at the door and shambled outside.

"McGregor," I croaked, spotting the foreman glowering at his phone with a couple of his men, "what's going on? Finished already?"

"You could say that," McGregor said, his scowl deepening.

"What's happened?"

"A fair bit, it looks like," he said, pocketing his phone and waving at his men to hurry up.

"What are you talking about?"

"We're terminating the contract."

I blinked. "You're what? Why?"

"Let's just call it…irreconcilable differences?"

I glared while I tried to get my brain to cooperate. "I don't understand."

"Let's not have a scene, sir."

"I'll take this up with Mr. Byrnes," I said, my voice rising.

"Mr. Byrnes' orders, *my lord*," he replied with a sneer, then turned his back and walked away.

I watched the men remove scaffolding and load equipment, sending grim looks my way as they did so. I hurried to the workshop forecourt to find a mobile phone signal. There was a missed call and an unpunctuated text message from Clem.

have u seen the news

My guts filled with ice. I tried to load my browser, but the internet signal wasn't strong enough. I returned to the house, hovered around the Wi-Fi router in the hall and loaded the *BBC News* website.

The Blood Winter Conspiracy — Cover-Ups, Manipulation and Deceit.

I blinked until the text became clear again. I read the article in a daze, my aching head spinning.

This groundbreaking report from Jason Singh, investigative journalist and haemophile-rights activist, details extraordinary revelations surrounding the true events of Blood Winter…

"...Ivor Novák has been woefully misguided in his decision to withhold the true aftermath of those terrible events. It is now imperative that haemophiles in the UK demand new representation..."

Singh goes on to comment about this unprecedented misrepresentation of facts...

...Haemophile Terje Kristiansen's survival...

...Untold damage to the public trust...

...Lord Aviemore's complicity...

...Legal counsel for Jon Ogdell, the man convicted of Terje Kristiansen's murder, has issued a statement saying they will be launching an appeal...

...Concerns growing over the fugitive Evgeniya Morak, who is now believed to be tied up in Novák's decision to withhold the truth...

...Support is growing for the Brassingtons and the 'Humans First' party after their announcement to run for parliament...

...Calls for those involved in the cover-up to be held to account and for Ivor Novák and Terje Kristiansen to be face charges at the Specialist Haemophile Criminal Court in Moscow...

I grabbed a table until the dizziness passed. Nausea rolled through me like salt water.

Novák's office tried to call me. I didn't answer. I tried to call Jay. He didn't answer.

I sat in the kitchen, staring at an untouched cup of coffee, my head swirling, guts quaking, waiting for the noise to stop. Even when the rumble of the builders' vehicles had died away, I didn't move. I felt like if I took even a small step, the house would come crashing down around my ears.

It was only when the sound of someone hammering on the side door filtered through to me that I came back to reality. I drifted through the house, feeling like I was moving through a nightmare. The stone passage was cold on my bare feet. The side door looked strange, as though it was from another time, another place. I opened it. Clem stood outside, his fist raised to knock again, clad in his usual attire of stained coveralls and a grim expression.

"Jesus, lad," he grumbled, "you look like you've seen the business end of a threshing machine."

"Do you need something?"

His beard twitched and he craned his neck to peer down the hall behind me. "So...is it...that haemophile..." He coughed. "Is *he* here?"

I rubbed my aching head. "No." He nodded, appearing to relax. "He wouldn't hurt you," I said, "even if he was."

"I know that." He looked uncomfortable, glancing at anything but me. "Just want this to stay between us. That's all."

"Want *what* to stay between us?" He shifted on his feet, glowering out over the hillside. When he still didn't speak, words rattled out of me instead. "I'm sorry I lied..."

He looked confused. "About what?"

"About him."

"Ain't none of my business, son," he said. "No reason for you to tell me who yer shackin' up with."

I raised my eyebrows. "Some people would consider it polite to let them know there's a vampire living just up the road."

"Ain't no such thing."

I smiled despite myself. "So have you come to hand in your notice or what?"

"You're too clever by half and yet dumb as shit sometimes, boy," he grumbled. "I came to see if you were all right."

I clutched the doorframe. "Why?"

"Shit's hit the fan," he said. "It's on the radio. Everywhere. Now, personally, I don't consider this—whatever it is—anyone else's business. But the hoo-hah? You'd think the world was ending. And you're in the bloody middle of it all again."

"I guess I must have been a prized wanker in a previous life."

"And some of this one too. Got too much of your dad in you some days, though not so much recently, thank God." I eyed him carefully. He twisted his fingers. "Just promise me one thing."

"What's that."

"Promise me you're not with this…this *haemophile* just for his…you know."

"His what?"

"You know what I mean."

I sighed, stared at the grass around his feet. "I'm not a Blood addict, Clem—though at this moment I'm not sure that wouldn't be easier to deal with."

"Don't joke," he said, examining my face. "And do us both a favor and stop the drinking. You hear?"

I sighed. "Clem, I appreciate your concern, but—"

"Concern my arse," he snapped. "This is experience speaking, laddie. Years of it. Years of watching people destroy themselves over nothing."

"Nothing?"

"Nothing is worth drinking yourself to death over, lad. *Nothing*. Understand?" I stared at the sky rather than meet his gaze. "You'll get through this. The tide'll turn again. It always does."

"Thanks, Clem. I…" I stumbled and managed a tight smile. "Thanks."

"Thank me by keeping it together," he said, prodding me in the chest. "I'm too old to run this business on my own, you hear me?"

"I hear you."

"Yer all I've got left of him. I won't live through all that again." He blinked, like he'd surprised himself by saying it out loud. He looked awkward but when I didn't respond, his round frame appeared to relax. He craned his neck to examine the house. "Fixed this place up nice, they did."

"They left this morning because of the news. They refuse to finish."

"Ah, there's not much left to do. Some new slates on the west wing is it. I could do that for ya, while it's dry."

"You could?"

"Aye," he said gruffly, shoving his hands in his pockets. "Used to do all sorts of odd jobs around here. And they've left the slate." He nodded to the pallets sitting by one of the outbuildings. "Still got my old ladders in one of these garages somewhere."

"That would be great."

"That's sorted then," he said with a nod, turning back down the track.

"You know the front door works now, right?" I called as he walked away.

"Too old to change habits now, lad."

Then he was gone. My head still pounded and my mouth still tasted sour, but my thoughts began to calm, like a sea leveling after a storm.

Terje would be back. Maybe I could persuade him go away with me for a while, escape to somewhere even more remote—Scandinavia, maybe Norway. He could show me where he came from, show me the mountains he'd grown up in. Maybe then we could finally work it out. Both Hati Nenge's and Jay's words still echoed in my head, but now I believed that if we were away from it all, then we'd be able to work it all out.

I loved him. I wanted to make him understand that that was enough for me. Forever.

I shelved the thought that 'forever' held a very different meaning for him and went upstairs.

I showered and brushed the hangover taste from my mouth, dressed in a clean T-shirt and jeans, brushed my wet hair back and shaved the scruff from my jaw. I went to the kitchen, drank cold water from the tap and raided the fridge then grilled bacon and black pudding, fried mushrooms and potato cakes and heated up some leftover haggis. I made a pot of strong coffee, filled the toaster with doorstep slices of bread and consumed it all with relish.

Whatever else had happened, whatever people might now think, the truth was out. Novák couldn't use us anymore. Neither could the Brassingtons. The world might be up in arms, but Clem was right. The next thing to be outraged about would soon fill social media and the news sites. People would eventually forget our faces, forget our names. The struggle for stability was far from over and was likely to get bloodier before it got better. But there really wasn't anything more we could do about it.

Surely, now Terje would feel the same way.

After I'd loaded the plates and pans into the dishwasher, I checked how many hours were left until sunset then did a circuit of the house, tidying, putting away clothes and boots, books and dirty glasses and cups that had started to build up on every surface. I changed the sheets on the bed, cleared the broken glass from the fireplace, cleaned out the decanter and packed it and the spare glasses away in a cupboard.

I made more coffee and sat in the drawing room, not putting on the television or looking at my phone.

It was as I was draining the cup that I heard a ringing. I frowned. My mobile was in my pocket and didn't receive calls in the house. It was the landline...the landline I'd had installed when I'd replaced the broadband and trusted the number to just one person...just one.

I hurried to the hall and picked up the handset.

"Meg?"

"Alec?" Her voice was shaking.

"Meg? What's wrong?"

"Help me, Alec. Please."

My veins filled with ice. "Where are you?"

"Please..." Her breathing was labored. "It's all gone wrong..."

"Meg?"

The call cut. I swore, checked the call history, but she'd rung from a withheld number. Panic spiked up my back. I tried to decide whether to ring the police, realized I didn't know what I'd say and wondered if they'd even help me if I did. For all I knew, they were on their way to arrest me already.

I took a steadying breath, looked up another number in my mobile contacts list and dialed, using the landline.

"Hello?"

"David?"

A pause. "Who is this?"

I braced myself. "It's Alec."

A heavy silence.

"Look... I know you don't want to speak to me."

"You've got that right."

"Just listen..."

"Listen? After all this? Never. Never again, Alec MacCarthy."

"David, it's Meg."

"You stay away from her, you hear me?" he snarled. "You've done enough."

"What do you mean?"

"Like you don't know."

"David, what's happened? Do you know where she is?"

"Like I'd tell you."

I fought impatience. "Look, arsehole... She's in trouble."

"Bloody right she's in trouble. Been MIA for over a week. Gone right off the bloody rails. Quit her job and left her husband, all because of you."

"*What?*"

"She's still in love with you, you moron." David's voice was tight with pain. "Loves you more than I ever did."

"That's not true."

"Goodbye, Alec. Don't call me again."

"David, wait. Meg's just this second called me. She sounded scared."

A pause. "What did she say?"

"Nothing. She just asked me to help her, then the call cut off. Do you know what's going on?"

"I told you —"

"She's not in love with me," I snapped. "She wouldn't throw everything away over me."

"That just shows how little you know about your ability to screw with people."

"I didn't—" I cut off the protest. "Just *think* a moment, David. This is not Meg. She doesn't do stuff like this. Something else is happening here, something bad."

"Like what?" he asked, sounding nervous now.

"You tell me. What's she been doing lately? Talking about?"

"Just her marriage falling apart."

"There must be something else, something out of the ordinary."

A noisy sigh. "She'd been going up to Glasgow…a lot."

"Glasgow?" Something twisted in my belly. "Why?"

"She was seeing someone. Brian found out."

I shook my head. It just didn't square with the Meg I remembered. "Did she actually *admit* to seeing someone?"

Another pause. "No."

"What did she *say* she was doing?"

"She wouldn't tell me or Brian… Just that it was important."

"Jesus Christ, David," I swore, hurrying to my laptop and booting it up. "And now she's disappeared? And you didn't try to find her?"

"Fuck you, Alec. You haven't seen her lately. She's been secretive, moody, frightened—textbook adultery behavior."

"Bollocks," I said, loading an old phone-tracing website and logging in. I sent up a quick prayer of thanks when I saw that Meg hadn't disconnected from the shared account we'd set up after uni. Neither had

David. His phone location pulsed over London, but Meg's wasn't pinging. "Shit."

"What is it?" Urgency now sharpened David's words.

"Her phone isn't registering on GPS. Hasn't for days. When she texted me the other day, it was from a different number."

"Shit."

"You didn't look for her yourself?"

"I thought she was crashing and burning," David argued. "No one can help you during that. You gotta hit rock bottom first. I learned that the hard way."

"You didn't even check to make sure she was safe?"

"Don't you dare judge me. You who lied to the entire world—"

"Not me. Novák."

"But you didn't think to set the record straight, did you? Not even with us? After everything that happened, you wouldn't even return our calls? Maybe if Meg had known you were holed up with your immortal fuck buddy instead of drinking yourself to death like your dad, she wouldn't—"

"Her phone last pinged a week ago," I cut him off.

"Where?" I swore. "Where, Alec?"

"The old distillery."

Silence. "Why the fuck would she go there?"

"I don't know."

"You have to get to Glasgow, Alec. The drive'll take me more than six hours."

"Don't come up," I said, shrugging into my jacket and searching for my car keys.

"Like hell..."

"You're angry," I said, as levelly as I could. "And she must have called me for a reason."

"She's *my* bloody sister."

"David, please," I begged. "If this is my fault, let me fix it."

"I can't just sit here."

"If you want to do something, call the police. Tell them your sister has been acting erratically and has now been missing for over a week."

"I already called them," he grated, "two days ago. They didn't take it seriously after Brian told them she'd left him for someone else. They'll take it even less seriously now that she's called you."

I swore again.

"Just get there, MacCarthy," he said. "And, I swear, if anything's happened to her—"

I cut the call.

Chapter Ten

I tried Meg's mobile over and over as I raced along the twisting country roads. It went straight to voicemail every time. The dense air split and burst into heavy, warm rain just as I reached the main road. I drove recklessly fast, skidding around the bends, overtaking other cars in a flash of spray. My chest was tight. My stomach had filled with concrete.

The last time I'd raced to Glasgow, along this very road, desperate to get to the derelict distillery before sunset was a clear memory. That time I'd been running from danger. This time it felt like I was running toward it. The loaded shotgun on the back seat didn't make me feel any more prepared.

I cursed Terje for keeping so much from me, for leaving me to face this alone. I cursed Novák for helping with one hand and taking away with the other. I cursed Hati Nenge for making me realize that, in their world, none of this mattered. They did what they did to protect themselves, to protect each other from a world that didn't accept them and probably never would.

Traffic slowed me then, three hours later, I crawled into the outskirts of the city. The rain washed over the windscreen and hammered on the roof. It was dark, despite it still being over an hour until sunset. Soon I was pulling up outside an exhaust-stained building with smashed windows and peeling fly posters pasted to the padlocked doors.

I retrieved the shotgun and crept around the back, up the stairs to the entrance to my old flat. The keypad was stiff but still opened to its code. I cracked the door and stood still, listening. All was silent. I nudged the door open with my gun. It creaked as it swung inward. I stood still. Nothing moved or made a sound.

When I crept in, the air smelled musty and damp. The shapes of the familiar, well-worn furniture gradually became visible in the gloom. Everything was as I'd left it that fateful winter night almost three years ago.

I made for the hall, my gun ready, straining my ears for any sound. I whispered Meg's name, but the flat appeared deserted, the rumpled bed linen and moldering shower curtain all undisturbed. I returned to the living area and stepped to the windows overlooking the distillery floor. The towering stills were just visible in the light bleeding in from the high windows. The shadows were silent and still between them.

It was then I noticed that the door to the storage basement stood open. I frowned, trying to remember if it had been open the last time I'd been there. I thought it had been locked for years…but I couldn't remember for sure. The prevailing memories I had from my last time here were not about the building.

I unbolted the door that led out onto a rickety iron stairway that spiraled down to the warehouse floor. The rusted iron creaked and cracked, and I winced with each noise, echoing loudly in the silence. I reached the bottom and held my breath, but there was no other sound. The air was musty, thick with the fug of rotten malt. I switched on my phone torch, scanned the floor and froze. The thick dust around the basement door had been disturbed. The padlock lay broken among the scuffed marks. I crept over and put my ear to the opening. All was quiet, but the silence had a different quality, like the air was holding its breath.

I pushed the door open. A low light lit the concrete stairwell. I put my phone away, my heart thumping against my ribs. I opened my mouth to call out but stopped myself, something in the air setting my skin crawling. I moved slowly so as not to make any sound, taking the stairs one at a time until I'd reached the bottom. The light was on in the storeroom. I crept to the window in the door and peered in.

The space was low-ceilinged but wide, with storage cells on either side. The cell at the far end was shut and bolted. I cracked the door and, finally, I heard something — a low keening, like someone in pain.

I padded forward, pressing my ear to the door of the bolted chamber. Another low, pained moan reached me through the wood.

"Meg?"

There was a moment of silence then her voice, barely recognizable, reached me through the wood. "Alec?"

I scrambled with the bolt, heaving at it with all my might, swearing when it wouldn't budge. It was heavy, stronger than anything that I'd ever seen when the distillery had been in use.

"Alec, please," came Meg's voice behind the door. "Get out of here. It isn't safe."

"Who did this to you, Meg?" I said, still tugging at the bolt.

"Alec, get out of here! *Now!*"

"You called me."

"She made me," she said, her voice high and cracking.

"She?" Finally, the bolt thunked back and I pulled open the door. Meg stood in the cramped space, her clothes rumpled and stained, her body rigid, her sloe-black eyes wide and bright with fear. Her dark skin was sallow. We stared at each other for a long, confused moment before I stepped forward.

"Don't," she warned, moving back. "Alec, please, don't come any closer."

"What happened?"

"Alec, please," she begged, wrapping her arms around herself, screwing her eyes shut and backing into the wall like she could crush herself through it. "I can...smell it."

"Smell what?" I murmured, though when she forced her black eyes open again, shining with desperate hunger, I knew.

"Your blood..." she whispered. "I can smell it. I can hear it."

I stepped closer. "Jesus... Meg..."

"Alec, *please*," she begged. "I don't want to hurt you..."

I stopped where I was. "How did this happen?" I said, my voice raw.

She slid down the wall, wrapped her arms around her knees and started to shake. My heart jerked around in my chest. I took a deep breath and reached for her.

"Come. Come with me. I'll get you out of here," I told her.

"I can't," she whimpered. "I can't go...out there, where people are."

"You can," I said, resting my hand on her trembling shoulder. She jerked her head up and grabbed my arm in a grip like iron. She drew her lips back from her teeth. Her eyes were blacker than space and her over-long canines glinted white against her deep-red mouth. I tried to pull away, but she was too strong. She pulled my arm toward her mouth but then, shaking, clenched her mouth shut and released me.

"Go," she sobbed. "Go, quick, Alec. I don't know how long I can—"

"Who did this to you?" I demanded.

"I'm so sorry..."

"What for?" I said, kneeling to meet her eyes but she wouldn't look at me.

"She said she just wanted to talk...that she wanted my help."

"*She?*"

"She said she'd turn herself in," Meg whispered, "but she wanted legal representation...*fair* representation. I agreed. I knew she would struggle to find it from anyone else. I thought I could help. She promised..."

"Meg, who are you talking about?"

She looked at me, her eyes blacker than the deepest winter night in the farthest reaches of the mountains. It was like she was seeing right into my soul. Then stared past me like she was seeing all her nightmares made flesh.

I was already turning when the blow fell.

* * * *

When I came to, my head was pounding like a hammer was beating the inside of my skull. When I could focus on anything other than the pain, I felt the pressure of bonds around my wrists and ankles. Then I heard Meg whimpering nearby.

I blinked my eyes open, swearing as the illumination from the strip lights stabbed through my brain. My phone and gun were nowhere in sight. I was bound to a chair with industrial twine. Meg was similarly restrained next to me, though with significantly more rope. Her fists were clenched so tightly that her nails had dug into her palms. Drops of dark blood, so dark it that it couldn't be human, spattered the arms of her chair and the concrete floor.

I tried to say her name, but my throat was raw and sore, and it came out as a croak. She jerked her head up, her eyes wide. She started to speak, but then a tall, pale figure stepped out of the shadows. Her eyes were the yellow of flame and shone like citrine. Her black hair had grown out and she'd tied it back, leaving the sharp angles of her face exposed. She smiled, revealing very white, very sharp teeth, the expression putting me in mind of a snake about to strike.

"Lord Aviemore, we meet again." Her voice rolled like piano music, low and lustrous but full of untapped power.

"Evgeniya…"

"Not quite the correct pronunciation," she said, stepping closer, "but close."

"What have you done to Meg?"

"Isn't it obvious?"

Meg was shaking harder, staring at the floor, breathing heavily through her mouth.

"You've turned her into one of you?" I said, my voice thin in my own ears.

"Nearly. She's got a way to go, but she's almost there."

"Why?"

"I have many reasons," she said, fetching a bowl and a knife from a table in the corner. "You don't need to know them all."

"She's in pain," I insisted. "She needs medical attention."

Evgeniya chuckled softly. "That's not what she needs."

Too quick for me to see, she lifted the knife and sliced into my forearm. I swore and tried to pull back, but the bonds were too tight. She held the bowl out to catch the trickling blood. Meg went rigid, her nostrils flaring. I called her name, but she seemed to be beyond hearing.

"Why are you doing this?" I said through clenched teeth as Evgeniya lifted the bowl to Meg's mouth. Meg leaned back, shaking even more violently, crushing her eyes shut.

"Drink, child," Evgeniya said softly. "It will help."

Meg tried to turn her face away, but Evgeniya tilted the bowl against her lips. She screwed her face up but then opened her mouth and drank, swallowing like someone dying of thirst finally given water. She relaxed, her brow smoothed and her face colored.

"There, dear," Evgeniya said, lowering the bowl and brushing the tendrils of sweaty hair back from Meg's face. "Better?"

Meg breathed deeply but didn't open her eyes.

"You won't get away with this," I snarled, "whatever this is. They'll find me. Terje will find me."

"That's what I'm counting on, little lord." I went cold. She frowned at my expression. "You needn't be frightened. I'm trying to help you...all of you."

"Mind explaining that one?"

She fetched a cloth and pressed it to the cut in my arm. She smiled at me, reminding me unpleasantly of a cobra assessing its prey. "We're all outcasts now, MacCarthy," she said softly. "The only option left is joining together."

"What are you talking about?"

"I'm making us a family. A home. I'm giving us each other, so we can be safe."

"You're...what?"

She sighed, tossing the cloth into the bowl. "Everything's so upside down now — registered communes, independent habitation, *licensed* reproduction?" She shook our head. "These are human terms, human restrictions. Our kind cannot live this way. We set our own rules, manage our own numbers and protection, always have. Novák has forgotten what that really means."

"So...what? You're starting a commune...with us?"

"I'm protecting my family, like I've always done." Her eyes glinted as her smile widened. "I'm giving you the chance to live forever...with Terje."

I stared. "You knew? That Terje survived?"

"Not right away," she said, examining her cut-glass fingernails. "It came to my attention when I came back to this country. He may be taking some awful chemical that stops me being able to find him...but our bond goes deeper than that. I sensed he was alive, even though I couldn't find him."

"So this," I said, nodding to Meg and the basement, "is to trap him?"

"To bring him back. Back to a family he can belong to."

"You're mad."

"You're telling me you wouldn't do the same?" she said, her face softening. "Wounded, melancholy Terje. He was always different. It was what made him so interesting...and why I could never bring myself to let him go, even though his differences cost me everything. But I should thank him, really. Being cast out has reminded me that the only world you can rely on is the one you build yourself."

"The residents at Forest Hill might beg to differ."

Her eyes glinted. "I can do no more for them. *Our* commune will be different—strong, self-reliant, no human rules, no restrictions. You don't want to be part of this broken world any more than I do. I'll give you to each other. And her," Evgeniya nodded at Meg. "Her brother too. And you'll all have me."

"This is all insane."

She laughed, a sound that seemed to come from the floor and out of the walls at once. "It's so sad that you can't see. But you will, my child. You will."

"Is it just because you can't stand being alone?"

"You say that like it's something to be ashamed of. No one survives alone."

"You won't get away with this."

"It's not a question of 'getting away' with anything. I will turn all the humans from Blood Winter. All the people that want things to be different. Then, together, we will show all humans, everywhere, that we will live by our own rules."

"That won't work. They're already hunting for you."

She laughed again. "Your human police force?" She snorted. "They won't even get close. And once I have you all ready, we'll be too strong for anyone. And when the Brassingtons put the rest of my plan into motion—"

I started. "The Brassingtons?"

"Oh, dear," she said, leaning her hands on the arms of her chair and pushing her face close to mine. "Do you think the humans arranged this all on their own?"

"You're the 'associate in Scotland'?"

She sneered. "Is that how they referred to me? Well, I'm not sure what I expected. Petulant, despicable cockroaches, the pair of them. But they have a purpose, like even the lowliest creatures on this earth. And I want you to remember, my lord, after all this is over, that I tried to do this for you peacefully. They made you that offer on my behalf. It's you who has made this difficult."

"But this isn't about me..." I stammered. "Those people? You're helping them stir up hatred against your own kind? Why?"

"Because my kind need to push back." Her voice had lowered. Her smile was gone. "They cannot go on as Novák and other elders have dictated, submitting to ridiculous restrictions just so that humans feel safe." She made a disparaging noise. "What about *us* feeling safe?" She shook her head. "The correct order needs to be reestablished. And for that, we need to be rallied to defend ourselves. That will happen once we prompt the humans show us their true colors. Then, when the time comes"—she ran a long finger down my cheek and jaw—"we will show them how strong we can be."

"And the Brassingtons are in on *that* part of the plan?"

"They are like most humans. They can't see past their own gain. But they will be the first to go." She smiled. "I'll keep them for you, if you like."

"I won't be part of this...and neither will Terje."

She touched her fingers to my ear, my hair, my neck, like she was memorizing every cell in my body. "I can offer you dozens of lifetimes with him—seeing everything as he does, feeling like he does for decades, centuries even. Imagine that, Alec," her breath was warm, her eyes burning. "Together, for all that time. Finally free."

"I won't be part of it," I said after a breathless hesitation.

"You will," she said, and sank her teeth into my neck.

Chapter Eleven

She locked me in the cell next to Meg's. The floor was hard and cold. My whole body ached with hunger and blood loss. The wound in my neck, though carefully dressed, burned and itched. Strange noises came from Meg's cell. I closed my ears, not wanting to think what the haemophile was doing to her with me unable to stop it.

Time became an unreal thing. The only thing to mark day dawning was Evgeniya's sudden absence. The only indicator of the hours that followed was increasing pain. I gave up kicking at the door when it became clear that I was doing more damage to my foot than the wood.

I knew night must have fallen again when I heard the bolt of Meg's cell being drawn. I yelled obscenities and threats through the concrete, but all was ominously quiet until the clunk of my own bolt being opened echoed in the cramped cell.

"She's nearly there," Evgeniya said, almost maternally, pulling her sleeve down over an already-healing wound in her wrist. "If she survives this stage, she will be fully transformed. Then it'll be your turn."

I tried to push her back, but she was too strong. She pulled the dressing from my neck and bit me again. The drawing sensation as she drank pulled at my fingertips and toes, threading pain through my flesh like hot wire. I shoved at her uselessly, my strength ebbing. By the time she was done, all I could do was lie on the floor and blink blearily at the ceiling.

She left again. I tried to talk to Meg, to tell her it was all going to be okay, that someone would find us and, somehow, they'd fix whatever Evgeniya had done to us. But my voice croaked, cracked and died in my throat. Meg didn't respond.

My stomach was a hard knot of hunger and my veins burned hollowly. My muscles felt like they had been individually stretched to their limit then pulled farther. The only things that were real were dizziness and confusion, pain and despair.

I was jerked out of a semi-conscious stupor by someone rattling at my cell door. I frowned, trying to focus. Evgeniya never had any trouble with the heavy bolt. Besides, by the eerie silence from the cell next door, I was sure it was still daytime.

There was a screech and a clunk, then the cell door opened. Light spilled in, making me blink and curse. Someone swore, then there were warm hands on me, sitting me up, and a familiar human smell of tobacco and mint shampoo.

"David?" I croaked.

"Jesus Christ, Alec," he said, voice shaking as he pulled my arm over his shoulder and helped me to my feet. "What the fuck happened?"

I tried to speak, but my throat was too dry. I staggered, trying to take my weight, and David, slighter than me, stumbled with me. Eventually he wrestled me out of the cell and lowered me into one of the chairs, then held a bottle of water to my lips. I drank greedily.

The water revived me a little and I could finally focus on the tight expression on David's face.

"I couldn't get you on the bloody phone. All day yesterday and this morning, I tried—"

"What time is it?" I rasped.

"What?"

I drank more water. "What *time* is it?"

David looked at his watch. "Nearly nine…"

I blinked. "Sunset?"

"Almost…"

"Meg," I croaked, trying to stand.

"What?" David looked around feverishly. "Where's Meg? She's here too?"

I nodded, gesturing at the other cell. David darted to the door and began heaving on the bolt. His shirt shifted and I noted the gun shoved into his waistband with only a fraction of the emotion I would have done at any other time. By the time I'd managed to shamble across the room, he'd gotten the bolt undone.

"Be careful," I said, clutching his arm.

"Why?" he asked, even though the heaviness in his expression told me he was reading his worst fear in my face. We opened the door together. Meg was curled on the floor in the corner, her face turned toward the wall. For a minute neither of us could move, then David knelt next to his sister and reached out a hand. I held my breath, but she didn't respond to his touch. He turned her over. Her eyes were closed. Her skin was clammy. Her dark curls stuck to her forehead. But her face was calm. Peaceful. I crushed my eyes shut as David reached out a shaking hand and pressed to fingers to her neck.

"She's alive," he said, voice shaking. I slumped against the wall, relief weakening my legs. "What's happened to her?"

I clutched at the doorframe to stay upright. "Evgeniya…"

David looked up sharply. "What?"

"Terje's former Magister."

"Yes, I know who she is," David hissed. "She's here?"

I nodded. "Somewhere. She was the one luring Meg here—to talk, she said. She promised she'd turn herself in if Meg agreed to represent her…"

David stared at me. "She was meeting…*her*? Why?"

"She thought she could help."

A number of emotions passed through David's eyes. "Why didn't she tell anyone?"

"Evgeniya swore her to secrecy. Meg thought she was negotiating the terms of her surrender…"

Tears brightened David's dark eyes. He swallowed and looked down at the too-still form of his sister.

"Is she…"

It took me a long moment to find my voice. "She's a haemophile…or very nearly… I'm not sure…"

David pressed a fist into his forehead and took a shaking breath. "How did it happen?"

"I don't know," I admitted.

David opened his eyes and weighed me up. "And you?"

"Not me…" I said. "At least…I don't think so. She's been…" I winced, rubbing at the dressing on my neck, the wound stinging and itching. "She drank from me. I think she was getting me ready."

"*Why*?"

"She's got some mad idea of building a commune with us...all of us."

"That's insane."

"I did tell her that," I said bleakly.

"Why you? Why Meg?"

"She said everyone from Blood Winter. I guess she thinks we all belong together..." David's face paled. "What?"

"Jon Ogdell was busted out of prison last night," he said in a low voice. "They suspect a haemophile attack..."

My blood ran cold. "We need to get out of here," I said. "Fast."

"For once I agree with you," David muttered and leaned down to shake Meg's shoulder. "Meg? Meg, it's me..."

Her face twitched, screwed up, then she bared her teeth, hissing. David backed away, shock slackening his face.

"Don't," I whispered urgently. "Don't try to wake her. Just cover her." I shrugged myself out of my bloodstained jacket. "Can you lift her?"

"Of course I can lift her," he said, sliding his arms under her. I draped the jacket over her face, tucked her hands underneath it and David lifted her from the ground. We moved, slowly, toward the door.

"What if they can't—"

David never got the chance to voice his fear. Evgeniya was in the doorway. She snatched Meg from David's grip like she was no more weight than a doll and shoved him back. He staggered into me and both of us went sprawling. I blinked through dizziness and swallowed the coppery taste in my mouth. David pulled his gun, but Evgeniya dragged him from the floor and pinned him to the wall by his throat.

"Right on time, Mr. Carlisle," she said, and sank her teeth into his neck.

I cried out. David made a strangled noise, dropping the gun and scrabbling uselessly at her vise-like grip. I got to my hands and knees, crawled closer, reached for the gun...

The was a noise like a rushing wind and David was slumping to the floor. There was a confused moment of breathless stillness, then I realized Evgeniya was against the wall, blood oozing from scratches across her face, her fingers digging into the concrete, glaring into the shadows of the door. I blinked a few more times but couldn't focus before Terje was attacking again. The air filled with bangs and crashes, flying feet and razor-tipped hands as they fought to overpower each other in the restricted space. I crawled to David and pulled him into my lap, attempting to staunch the bleeding from his neck. The wound had been ripped wide when Evgeniya had been torn away and his blood poured over my hands, soaking our clothes. He stared up at me, his eyes wide, mouth opening and closing.

"It's all right," I breathed, "It'll be all right, David. Just keep still."

"Meg?" he croaked

She lay sprawled in the doorway of her cell, raising her head to peer blearily at the chaos.

"She's okay," I assured him, clamping my hand harder over his wound. "It's all okay. Terje is here..."

Evgeniya screamed, loud enough to shake the glass in the door. There was another crash, then the haemophiles were standing, breathing hard, glaring at each other across the room, their clothing torn, scratches bleeding on both their faces and necks.

"You're faster," Evgeniya said.

"You're slower," Terje returned.

Evgeniya grinned. "You can't win, Terje. You know that."

"I'm not alone," Terje said. "Novák knows I was coming here. There will be others. Soon."

"This is all beginning to feel very familiar," Evgeniya said, glancing around us all, one at a time. "So how about, this time, you make the right decision?"

"And what's that?"

"Join me," she said, smiling a Blood-darkened smile. "We'll start a new commune, Terje, with all these humans you hold so dear. I will give them all to you if you join me."

Terje hesitated. His gaze landed on me, and for a horrifying second, I knew he was considering it. But then he shook his head. "No."

"You can't fight me forever," she said, approaching. Terje appeared to be fighting the urge to step back. "These humans and you are the representation of everything that is conflicted and divided between our kinds. But the war is coming. If we band together, fight side by side, our kind will be united again. And when the fighting is done, we can be safe, away from all this, with the freedom to exist as we want."

"You think I'd want that?"

"I *know* you do," she said softly.

David moaned in my lap, his eyelids flickering. "Terje," I said, my voice shaking.

"Ignore him," Evgeniya commanded. "His friend won't survive. There's no need to rush on his account.

However..." Evgeniya reached down and helped Meg to her feet. I clutched David closer, casting about, trying to find something more effective than my hand to staunch the wound, and spotted the gun just within reach. Meanwhile, Meg sagged in Evgeniya's grip, breathing hard, her eyes heavy, staring at Terje like she was trying to remember why he was significant. Terje's face hardened.

"What have you done?"

"Started our new family," Evgeniya whispered.

"That was not licensed." The shock evident on Terje's usually impassive face was palpable. "Did she even consent?"

Evgeniya lifted an eyebrow. "No. But only because she didn't understand what I'm offering."

"It's worse than if you'd killed her."

"You don't really think that," she said, lowering Meg into a chair.

"You don't see anything, do you?" Terje said. "*You're* the reason everything went so wrong—why we're hated, why they can't trust us." His pained gaze came back to me. I couldn't move. I begged him with my eyes. David was going still. I could smell his blood, feel the pain that stiffened his rigid body. I gripped him harder, trying to summon the strength to stand, to carry him out, to try to reach the gun, anything.

"I'm the only one who can bring you happiness," Evgeniya reasoned. "Peace. Security. You don't need anyone else."

"I need Alec."

I froze with my fingertips on the gun's handle. If I moved, David would shift and my grip on his wound would slip. If I didn't get the gun and try to do something about Evgeniya, he was going to bleed out anyway. But in that moment, all I was aware of was Terje.

"And you will have him," Evgeniya replied, like a patient parent lecturing a child. "I'll turn him for you."

"*No*," Terje said. "I love him as he is."

Fire rekindled in Evgeniya's eyes. My heart exploded behind my ribs. Meg blinked between us all and, slowly, her expression changed. Her grip tightened on the chair. She looked at me, then her eyes fell on David.

"You don't know what you're talking about," Evgeniya said. Meg slid onto her hands and knees and began to crawl toward the gun.

"I won't let you hurt him," Terje intoned.

Evgeniya gazed at him, her face still. "It's like you've gone backward—all the more reason to bring you into a commune as soon as possible."

"Why me?" Terje asked, more emotion than I'd ever heard him express straining his voice. "Why this fixation on *me*? On these humans? Why risk coming back, risk everything, just for me?"

"Because you never lost it, Terje," Evgeniya said, stepping close to him. Meg had almost reached the gun. Her face was tight, her fraught gaze flicking between her brother, Evgeniya and the firearm. "You never lost your humanity. It links you to this world. We need that balance to survive."

"They don't want this," Terje said in a low voice. "Alec doesn't want this."

"How do you know? Have you asked him?"

Terje looked at me. The surging of emotion in his eyes was like a storm out at sea. A hundred thousand things to think, say and feel tumbled over each other, but I couldn't even begin to fight them into order, let alone decide what they meant.

At that moment, Meg closed her fingers around the pistol and the metal scraped the concrete. Evgeniya turned, and in a flash it was gone, Meg thrown against the wall and David ripped from my arms.

"It's time you all learned about consequences," Evgeniya said. Terje lurched toward her, but he wasn't fast enough to stop her snapping David's neck.

Meg's cry drowned out my own and reverberated around the walls like an air-raid siren. David's lifeless body slumped to the floor. His eyes were wide and staring, fixed on me. My vision blurred, and I tasted bile. Meg flung herself at Evgeniya, but Terje thrust himself between them. The gun went flying. I tried to go after it, but the door slammed open and a dark shape, moving too fast to see, darted into the fray. Terje and Meg were flung back, and the pistol was scooped out of my reach.

With a crash hard enough to crack the brickwork, Evgeniya was slammed into the wall. I just had time to recognize the tall, coated figure of Hati Nenge when she brought the gun up, pressed the barrel to Evgeniya's forehead and fired.

The silence that followed was more deafening than the shot itself. Evgeniya thudded to the floor, a neat hole, oozing black, above her right eyebrow. Her mouth was open. The fire in her yellow eyes had gone cold.

"Sorry I'm late," Nenge said.

"She's…dead?" I croaked.

"Oh yes," Nenge said, pocketing the gun. She surveyed the scene with a crease between her eyebrows. "Dear, dear, what a mess."

I scanned the room. Terje, cut and bloodied, stood staring at Evgeniya's body like he couldn't quite understand what he was seeing. At his feet lay the bent and broken form of David, soaked in blood, his eyes dull. Meg, whimpering, knelt next to her brother and gathered him into her arms. His head lolled sickeningly on her shoulder. She sobbed.

I tried to get to my feet. It broke whatever spell was holding Terje still and he was at my side in an instant.

"Alec," he breathed, holding me up and looking earnestly into my face, "you're hurt."

"I'm alive," I rasped.

"I'm so sorry," he said, his voice so choked that I felt for sure he was about to cry. "So sorry."

I brushed the hair from his face with a shaking hand. My throat wouldn't open to allow speech. I put my arms around his neck, rested my face in his hair and let the shaking take me. He wound his arms around me in turn and held me tight.

"How did you know?" I whispered.

"I got home, and you weren't there. I checked the call history. David told me where you'd gone." He was silent for a moment. "I told him not to come...but day was near. I couldn't get here faster..."

I clutched him tighter.

"We need to get you to a hospital," he murmured into my hair.

"Did you mean it?"

"Mean what?"

"You know what."

He pulled back and looked into my face. His lips were pale, his eyes shining. "Of course I meant it."

I kissed him. He tasted like home.

Epilogue

We crested the ridge together. The sky arched, inky black and studded with stars, so high above that it felt like we could fall off into it. Their light, combined with a full moon, made it easy for me to see my way without a torch, but Terje, as always, was close at my side to guide me if I mis-stepped. We gazed down into the night-silent glen, the lighted windows of Glenroe glowing in the dark. It looked truly beautiful. By day, with its sand-blasted stonework, new roof, doors and window frames, its glory came close to what it must have been in its medieval heyday. At night, under the starlight, it looked like a fairytale castle, somewhere in another world, protected by remoteness and magic.

Terje slipped his fingers into mine.

It had been a long, hard few months, but finally, as the sultry, wet autumn was starting to surrender to the chill of winter, I felt like we were finally coming out the other side.

I'd spent almost a week in a specialist hospital in London after being rescued from the distillery.

Physically, it was nothing that a few blood transfusions and nutrient drips couldn't fix. But the shock of it all—watching David die, nearly dying myself, seeing Meg forced into something like living death—had sunk deep into my bones and brain and overloaded me. They'd kept me sedated for three days, bringing me around with great care and only when a counselor was on hand.

Not that I wanted to talk about any of it—or at least not with a stranger.

Terje wasn't allowed to visit me. I received dribs and drabs of news over the hospital's unreliable Wi-Fi. The downside to Evgeniya's actions was, predictably, more negative press for the haemophile community. The significant upside was that her links to Jon Ogdell and the Brassingtons had been exposed, along with their joint plan to provoke riots and violence. The Brassingtons had been jailed without bail, along with most of their inner circle of supporters, and public opinion, minus a few vocal exceptions, was shifting, glacially, back toward the hope of a peaceful co-existence.

The fact that Evgeniya had been stopped by other haemophiles certainly didn't hurt the publicity campaign.

But Terje, Novák and Nenge all had things to answer for, as did I. Three different detectives interviewed me over the course of my week in the hospital. And while that investigation was going on, no one, haemophile or human, was allowed into my room.

Finally, on the seventh night, I woke with the strength to stand on my own. I was all for discharging myself immediately but, as if sensing it, that moment was when Hati Nenge appeared at my bedside.

"Lord Aviemore," she said, a faint smile on her face. "You look better."

"What are you doing here?"

"The human queries are completed, so Novák sent me to check on you."

"Better late than never."

Her expression didn't shift. "I'm assuming that is a barbed remark about my late appearance at the distillery, to which I will just say in my defense that you weren't supposed to run off in the middle of the day without telling anyone where you were going. I found you in time, didn't I?"

Too late for David. I swallowed at the kick of pain.

She looked away. "Yes. Sorry about your friend."

"No, you're not."

She shrugged, looking about the room with an uncertain expression. "The nature of human bonds is lost on me, I'm afraid. But I know they're important. So, before I go…" She moved to the door and opened it. Meg stepped into the room. I sat up. She came forward, moving slowly, almost stiffly, like she was in pain.

"Hey," she said, with an odd, twisted smile that seemed to be trying to hide her teeth.

"Meg? You're okay?"

"I'm…" She smiled strangely again and perched on the chair next to the bed. "I was going to say 'fine', but that's not really true."

Her rich, dark skin which had previously glowed with human warmth now shone with an ethereal, pearlescent glow. Her eyes looked larger, and she appeared to have lost weight. Her cheekbones were more prominent, the lines of her jaw sharper. Her hand, when she took mine, was cool.

"How do you feel?" I said.

"I should be asking you that."

"Meg…"

Her jaw tightened. "Hungry. Angry. Terrified."

I crushed her hand tight. "I'm so sorry."

She squeezed back. "So am I."

"There's nothing they can do?"

Meg glanced at Nenge, who was standing in the corner, then back at me. "No."

I squeezed her hand tighter, words failing me.

"At least now Brian believes I wasn't cheating on him." Her smile was bleak.

"That's…good?"

"We're giving it another go." She looked at our joined hands for a long moment. "Perhaps you can give me some tips."

I covered our hands with my free one. "You don't need any. If he loves you, that's all that matters."

She let out a shuddering sigh. "Novák's helping me get registered, at least, to make everything legal. So that's one less thing to worry about." She raised her head, looking a little stronger. "I'm joining his legal team."

"After everything that has happened?"

Her expression grew even more serious. "Evgeniya was lost, Alec, let down by a world that left her isolated and angry. She needed help, not judgment. That's the reason I agreed to meet her in the first place."

"She turned you. She killed David. She engineered a situation that could have ended in mass murder and riots…"

"I'm doing what I'm doing now so that no one, human or haemophile, ever feels like that is a solution again."

When I looked into her eyes, I knew she could do it, too.

"David's funeral is tomorrow," she said after a long silence. "Think you can make it?"

I swallowed until my throat cleared. "Yes. Even if I have to break out of here, I'll be there."

"He didn't deserve this," she murmured. "After he fought so hard to get his life back... To have it taken from him like that..."

"He was protecting you...both of us."

She nodded stiffly. "I know. He always did — or tried to."

"Mrs. Daile...Meg." Nenge stepped forward, gesturing at the door. "We should be going."

Meg's expression flattened. "She means I'm due a feed," Meg said. "I tell you... Eternal youth and unbounded physical power are one thing, but the reality of it is really rather disgusting."

"I don't complain about *your* food," Nenge said, casting a disparaging glance at my hospital tray, which still contained the remnants of a questionable cottage pie.

"This doesn't count," I muttered.

"The management of newborns is strictly monitored," Nenge went on flatly. "We're required to regulate your feed and rest by law. The processes are monitored for a reason."

"Yes, yes," Meg said. "Honestly, Hati, you're worse than Novák."

"Meg, before you go," I said, grabbing her hand. "What's happening with Terje?"

"We've been cleared of any charges relating what happened in Glasgow." Meg glanced at the unreadable expression on Nenge's face then back at me. "But Terje is answering questions about everything else. There's to be a formal inquest into the cover-up, the Brassingtons, all of it."

"And Jon Ogdell?"

"Dead."

I stared. "I didn't see that anywhere."

"It's not been publicly announced yet. Evgeniya broke him out of prison and started the process of turning him. But then she was killed. By the time someone found where she'd hidden him, he'd died of blood loss."

"That needs to come out," I said, once my voice was working again. "All of it. Jay's article has already set everything against Novák. If he lies again…"

Meg laughed softly. "Why, Alec MacCarthy… Expressing opinions on contemporary social and political issues?"

"It seems I have to, or they come back to bite me in the arse."

"Well, don't worry," Meg said. "It's not going to be covered up. Novák is working with Scotland Yard and the Home Office to run the inquest. All the questions will be answered. That's what Terje is helping them prepare for. It looks like no one is facing formal charges, but they do need his co-operation. He's agreed, with some conditions."

"Conditions?"

"He has asked that, once this is over, he be freed from any future obligations — to Novák, to anyone."

I stared at her, something light and warm swelling in my chest.

"Of course I meant it."

"That's…" I swallowed. "That's good."

"It is," she said, with a more genuine smile. But then her face fell. "Though Jason Singh disagrees."

I blanched. "Jay?"

"Yes. He's changed since you were at uni, hasn't he?" she said thoughtfully. "But then, I suppose we all have."

I didn't know what to say until I saw the sparkle of humor in her eye. "Can't deny that."

She brushed her fingers against the cover, staring like she was momentarily lost in the feel of the rough fabric. "Jay thinks Terje is so central to the scandal that it's imperative he be seen to be punished. Personally, I think he's just a bit messed up by all this." She lifted her gaze to mine and smiled. "Not that anyone can blame him."

I glanced at Nenge. "Could we have a moment?" She stared at me uncomprehendingly. "In private?"

She blinked then made for the door. "Three minutes, Mrs. Daile."

When we were alone, it took me almost all the first minute to find words. "Do you love me?"

She looked confused. "Of course I do."

"I don't mean as a friend."

Her eyebrows drew together. There was hurt but also exasperation in her eyes. "Alec, really?"

"David said—"

"David thought I was pining over you because *he* was."

I blinked. "What?"

"You didn't know?"

I shook my head dumbly.

"Oh, Alec," she said, sitting on the bed, "you really don't realize what you're like, do you?"

I felt sick again. "What am I like?"

"You're"—she raised her hands, seemingly searching for a word—"extraordinary."

"That's just a nice way of saying 'a fucking nightmare'."

She gave me a baleful look. "That's what Terje thinks, is it?"

"Sometimes." My smile was thin. Hers was warmer. I looked away. "But seriously, that's why I'm asking you…"

"Alec—"

"I think I've hurt you…*know* I've hurt you, more than I can ever make up for. I've avoided you rather than face it. I know I've apologized before, but not enough. I am sorry, Meg. *Really* sorry."

She sighed with a sad smile. "You have nothing to be sorry for, Alec. You're right. I had feelings for you once, possibly more recently than I allow myself to admit." She rested her cool hand on my suddenly hot face. "But that wasn't your fault. It wasn't mine either. Love just…does its own thing. We both know that— better than most, probably."

"Yes," I said, half bitter, half jubilant.

"And I love you still. But I hope I don't hurt your feelings when I tell you that I love my husband more."

Something lifted in my chest. "No. No, that's good. That's as it should be."

"I know."

"David just scared me, I guess."

"David was good at projection." She lowered her eyes. "Too good."

We were silent for a while, then she kissed me on the cheek. "Goodbye, Alec. See you tomorrow."

* * * *

I discharged myself the next evening to attend David's night-time funeral. Meg collected me from the hospital just after sunset. She didn't speak on the drive to the crematorium. I knew there was nothing to say, so I didn't attempt to break the silence. It was a cold, wet evening for August—damp, with no moon.

A surprising number of haemophiles attended, including Novák, though I suspected they were there more to show public support for Meg as their new legal representative than for any genuine feeling for the loss of her brother. Jay was there too but kept a careful distance from everyone.

The physical strain of being out of bed caused my head to start spinning toward the end of the service. But when Terje appeared silently at my side, threading his fingers through mine, I felt like I could climb mountains in a single bound.

His touch anchored everything. It took the fight out of me and allowed me to confront the true extent of what I was feeling. As the coffin rolled out of sight behind a velvet curtain, something broke in me that I wasn't sure would ever be whole again. My throat closed over. The tears flowed.

When the service ended and Terje announced to Novák that he was taking me home, the emotions, like waves at the edge of a stormy sea, started to ebb. He took me out into a cold, drizzly evening. The droplets that caught in his hair winked like gems under the carpark floodlights. He drew me into the shadows, away from the other people trickling out from the service and pulled me into an embrace. I clung to him so hard that I knew it must be hurting, but my legs were weak, my joints ached, and in that moment, I felt that the only strength I had left was what allowed me to hold on to him.

"It's over?"

He drew his head back to look into my eyes. He looked tired but his eyes were bright. "It's over."

"How?"

He brushed strands of damp hair out my face with a contemplative air. "I answered their questions. I explained our reasoning. They accepted it. The media storm will take a while to blow out, but it won't touch us at Glenroe."

"Are you sure?"

"Things are changing—or being more accepted where they cannot be changed."

I blinked, the grief and physical exhaustion tugging on my senses, making them sluggish. "So, what is actually happening?"

"Nothing that need concern us," Terje said, glancing over his shoulder at the small knots of people gathering to talk softly under umbrellas. "Novák still has some rough road ahead of him, but he's traveled worse. But it's been mutually agreed that you and I are now…surplus to any requirements."

I swallowed. My throat was tight, my heart jerking about behind my ribs like the mechanism of a malfunctioning clock. Meg was standing not too far away, her face pale and set, shaking hands with dozens of people, human and haemophile, who had no idea what she was going through. Brian stood at her side, his eyes wary as he nodded to all who came to offer condolences.

Meg's eyes were bright but dry, the ethereal haemophile glint to their depths making her pain glow like a deep, dark fire. She suddenly seemed very far away. I didn't know if I could bridge that gap any more than anyone else—or even if she would want me to. Then Novák emerged and drew her aside for a quiet conversation. They both fell silent as Jay left the building, his head bowed, heading for the carpark. But I didn't look away from the grieving Meg, her unnerved husband or the large haemophile who, even now, was doing everything he thought necessary to make things better for all of us.

The gulfs between us were deep, wrought by pain and fear and misunderstanding, and yet I sensed the unbreakable threads linking us all.

I looked into Terje's clear, silver eyes, watching me like he was watching my thoughts, and suddenly understood everything he had been trying to tell me.

"Thank you," I whispered.

"For what?"

"For everything," I said. "And for coming here tonight."

"Of course. I'm so sorry about David. I know he meant a lot to you."

I nodded, sniffing.

"You want to go home?"

"More than I can say."

"Do you want to say goodbye first?"

I glanced at Meg, moving slowly toward her car, Brian's hand on her back, her face dazed and exhausted and shook my head. "I'll ring her tomorrow."

"Good," he replied. He took my hand and led me to our car. I smiled at the sight of it, the dark green almost black under the floodlights, but frowned when Terje didn't open the driver's door. He was staring over my shoulder.

I turned. Jay stood under the trees at the entrance to the Memorial Garden. He was watching us, his face drawn in the dim light.

"Talk to him," Terje said.

"I don't want to."

"You'll regret it if you don't."

I frowned. "This is all his fault. If he hadn't written that damn article—"

"He was hurting." I looked at him in surprise and the suggestion of a smile played about his mouth. "Come on, Alec. Give me some credit."

I felt an argument hovering in the air about how Terje seemed to understand the nuances of human emotion just fine when it suited him. But I didn't want to argue—not again, not today.

"I've got nothing to say to him."

"Alec"—Terje brushed a knuckle along my jaw—"it's time to stop running away from your problems."

I blanched and opened my mouth to protest, but Terje climbed into the car and shut the door.

I hesitated, my hand on the passenger door handle, then turned and ambled slowly across the dark, wet carpark.

"Alec," Jay said as I joined him, his voice sounding tortured, low and unfamiliar, "I was hoping to speak to you."

"You were, huh?"

He swallowed, eyes bright, jaw clenched. "I wanted say I'm sorry."

"It's a bit late for that," I said, though my voice was more weary than angry.

He frowned. "I'm not talking about the article."

"About what, then?"

"About David," he said exasperatedly. "And Meg. And what happened to you."

I stared at the wet tarmac between us. "Why'd you do it, Jay?"

"Because it was the right thing to do."

"You only blew the whistle to get back at me…and at Terje."

His face flushed but his voice was controlled, "You really think I'm that petty?"

"Aren't you?"

His face paled with emotion. "You were caught up in the lie, like everyone else. It had to come out for everyone's sake."

"And what did Novák think of that reasoning?"

Jay looked away. "Novák made a serious error of judgment—and it's not the first. It's time for change."

"And you're that change, is that it?" I said, watching the last of the other guests' cars drive away, leaving an eerie silence behind.

"I'm campaigning to be elected as the UK representative to the new International Assembly for Haemophile Affairs. They need a human to educate humans. I can do that. And a lot of their kind agree."

"So no regrets at all?" I said, and my voice sounded raw, even to myself.

"It's time for honesty. Progress."

"David died, Jay."

"Not because of what I said," he said, a little too defensively. "Because secrets were kept in the first place, Evgeniya Morak lost faith in the system. If Novák had just told the truth, there would be more trust between our kinds. The likes of the Brassingtons would never have been able to—" He broke off, glaring into the shadows. Finally, he looked at me again. "I'm sorry." He said it more sincerely this time. "I know none of this matters to you, and I know I let my personal feelings interfere. But everything I said about you and Terje is true—and all this just proves it."

"You're wrong."

"Fine. I wish you luck, I really do. I just hope yours isn't the next funeral I attend."

"You're being over-dramatic."

"Am I?" His face was hard. "How many people have died since you met him? Huh? How many?"

I stopped myself from counting and glanced back at the car. Terje was looking at his phone, but I knew he could hear every word. I turned back to Jay.

"You're right, Jay. He is dangerous. They all are. And it's important there are people like you out there, helping us to understand that. But Terje and me? We belong together. We understand each other better than anyone of our own kinds can."

He let out a shuddering breath and seemed to shrink. "Just tell me one thing, Alec," he said quietly, "before we say goodbye."

I sighed. "Go on."

"Why did you sleep with me?"

I winced.

"Tell me, please. And no 'caught in the moment' crap. You needed it, the way someone grieving needs to be reminded that they're still alive. Why were you grieving when he never died?"

I scuffed the tarmac with my food. "We'd...hit a rough patch, I admit. But we're through that now."

"Just like that?"

I frowned. "It took some work and will take some more, I think. But I...understand things better now."

"So that was why? You'd hit a 'rough' patch? That was why you needed me that day?"

I sighed. "Don't make me say it, Jay."

"Say what?"

I rubbed my face. His face was very still in the dark. Raindrops sparkled in his hair, jeweling the shoulders of his jacket. I made myself hold his gaze as I spoke. "The truth is…"

"Yes?"

I looked away. "He told me to sleep with you."

"*What*?"

"Terje *told* me to do it," I said, shame billowing through my insides like nausea.

He frowned. "Excuse me?"

I chewed my lip. "At the time, he thought it would be…good for me, or something, to sleep with humans once in a while. I was so angry, so confused. I…" I inhaled deeply and looked up at the dark sky. "I did need it. And I did want it, want you. After Forest Hill, after what Bonny had said, I wondered if we ever could have a future and…yes, I wanted comfort. That's what I told myself. But, under it all…I think I hoped he'd find out. I hoped it would make him react, even though he told me it wouldn't." I took a deep, shuddering breath. "And it did make him react, though not in the way I'd hoped. That was never going to happen. I realize that now. But, either way…I took advantage of you. That was very wrong. I'm sorry."

Jay's face was drawn, his lips pale. Pain filled his eyes and I made myself take it in, knowing I'd caused it.

"I would have made you happy, Alec," he said after a long, pained silence. "I know you've not had the best of luck with men, but with me…" I watched him take a breath, and when he spoke, his voice was steadier. "I'm different. I understand you. And I would never have hurt you the way he has…the way he will. Remember that."

He turned and strode off into the night.

* * * *

I was confined to bed with the unwelcome thoughts Jay had planted for some time after returning to Glenroe and still weak for days after that, despite the combined efforts of Terje and Clem to make sure I ate properly. But, slowly, as the days crept by, the phone didn't ring and the doorbell didn't chime, I began to believe that Novák would keep his promise this time — and so would Terje. My appetite returned and, with it, my strength.

I kept in touch with Meg. I finally acknowledged how much I'd missed her. I thought she'd been part of a life I'd wanted to leave behind. Now I realized how both naive and selfish that had been. Meg had never wanted anything from me but my friendship and for me to be happy. And, finally, I felt I was on firm enough footing to want the same things for her.

She never mentioned anything about the wider world unless I asked, but I knew she was making waves in her new position.

She certainly had her work cut out for her. Novák continued to staunchly defend his previous decisions surrounding the aftermath of Blood Winter, stating that his motivation had been solely to protect Terje and myself. Gradually, with a considerable amount of help from Meg, and even, eventually, from the newly elected UK Rep to the NAHA Jason Singh, Novák reclaimed his position as a trusted public figure. He continued to fight politically to protect and integrate haemophiles peaceably into the UK. I suspected he still used tactics that weren't strictly legal and that the NAHA and UK Government would officially denounce should they ever come to light. But, as far as I was concerned, if it was working, who were we to question?

And it did appear to be working. Violence was down and protests were less frequent. Hate speech online was being denounced and policed, and I thought, even just a few short months after David and Evgeniya had been killed, that I could see progress being made — when I cared to look at all... which wasn't often.

During my calls to Meg, I usually asked after Brian, her life and her friends. We spoke often and sometimes she made the all-day drive up to Glenroe to stay a few days. Brian eventually came too, finally starting to look at me with something approaching human feeling in his eyes.

It was like Meg and I were kids again, sharing fears and triumphs and dreams and never letting too much reality bleed into the simple joy of conversing with someone who has known you all their life.

Some things were different, of course. David was gone and so was she, in a way. Her life as she'd known it was over. She was holding on to her marriage, but she knew she was going to watch the world change around her, for good or ill, while she just... continued. Haemophiles weren't immortal. I remembered Terje accusing me of having read too much Anne Rice when I'd asked him about it when we'd first met. Eventually, death came for everyone in some shape or form. But how many human lifetimes would elapse before that would happen to Meg, it was impossible to guess.

Meg knew that she would live so long that one day she probably wouldn't remember Brian, or me — or any of the things that had been important to her as a human. I sensed she was mourning those things even before they were gone, just as much as she was mourning David. For that, and for the simple reason that I had finally admitted how much I loved her, I was glad to stay in touch.

She spoke to Terje almost as much as she spoke to me. He was polite and understanding, but I could tell he was deeply affected by what his Magister had done to her. He answered the questions as best he could that she didn't feel she could ask Novák, though a lot of the complexities of haemophile existence were a mystery, even to them. But they found comfort in each other in their own way.

I was happy for both of them, not least because I now understood that, sometimes, Terje needed to talk to someone like him, especially when that someone had shared so much of what had brought us together.

And so it was, that late autumn night, as we stood with the cold wind whipping through our hair, looking down on our home and hearing nothing but the silent night around us, that Terje surprised me by breaking the silence first.

"I'm sorry, Alec," he said softly.

"For what?"

"I told you it was time to stop running away from your problems. I can't ask that from you if I don't intend to do the same."

A chill went through me. "What problems, Terje?"

He stared into the dark, face hard. "I've been meaning to tell you, for a long time, that you were right about me—when you said I was holding back, that I was keeping myself from you."

The chill spread further. "How do you mean?"

He let go of my hand. Cold rushed between us. I had the sickening sensation of teetering on the edge of a cliff, about to fall, but then I saw that he was searching in his pocket. He withdrew a small, worn leather pouch.

"I've been carrying this around for months," he murmured, opening it. He tipped something out onto his palm. The polished metal glinted coolly in the starlight. It was a ring, solid silver, perhaps...or white gold. It was the same shade as his eyes, and it sent something hot chasing the cold out of me.

"This belonged to someone important to me," he continued, "from my previous life. I can't remember how or why. I don't even remember their name, just that they were important." He looked up. For the first time since I'd known him, he looked nervous. "Some things linger from the life before. And where I grew up...this is what you did to show someone that you loved them, that they were important to you and that you wanted to spend the rest of your lives together."

So slowly that I wasn't even sure what I was seeing, Terje held the ring out to me. "Haemophiles...we don't do this. Get married, I mean." I blinked until the rushing in my ears subsided. He continued softly, watching my face. "We live too long to promise our lives to anyone. Besides, our communes are our family...at least they're supposed to be. So, we don't marry each other or partner in a way that a human would recognize."

He took my hand. His voice changed, like emotion was choking him. "But when I found you, Alec, I found that I missed it."

"Terje," I started, my voice sounding distant and strange over the rushing in my ears. But he spoke over me.

"You saved my life, Alec. And I don't mean when you helped me in Jon Ogdell's basement." He swallowed and I held my tongue with a monumental effort, knowing he wasn't done. "I was lost before I met you. And I'm not an idiot," he went on, voice tight. "I know we can't have anything…real. Anything legally recognized, I mean. But" — he took a breath — "I want to marry you, Alec, in our own way. I've wanted it for a long time."

The words sank into me, heating me through from soul to skin, but I couldn't rid myself of the damp fog of confusion threatening to swamp the glow.

"But you always said it would never last," I murmured. "You pushed me away. You said — "

"It wasn't because I didn't love you," he insisted. "Everything I said about our differences, the obstacles…? For any other human, it would be true. But it isn't…" He took a breath. "It isn't with you."

"So why did say all that?" I almost whimpered, joy and pain both heavy in my chest. "Why did you make me believe that one day it would all be over?"

"Because one day you'll die." His grip on my hand tightened. "How could I possibly make this promise, allow myself to feel these things, knowing that one day you'll be gone…and I'll have to go on without you?"

He held the ring between us. I held his hand tightly, gripping his arm hard with my other hand so he could feel me and know I was trembling.

"I...I don't know," I said, miserably.

He kissed me. There was a dampness of tears against my cheek. He held me against him, crushing his hand and the ring between us. Eventually, he pulled away, pressed his forehead to mine and held me still.

"I'll turn you," he whispered, so quiet that his words were almost whisked away on the wind. "If you ask me, I'll turn you."

"Turn me? Into...into a haemophile?"

He nodded. "It will hurt. It'll take time. But once it's done...we can face a longer future together."

I groped for understanding. "Are you even allowed to?"

"No," he said. "I'm not licensed. We'd have to go into hiding. But I'd do it, if you asked me."

"Is...is that what you want?"

He was silent. He didn't even appear to be breathing. "What do *you* want?" he asked.

I looked into his eyes. "I love you, Terje," I said, the words so full that I almost went to my knees with the amount it took out of me to finally utter them. "If we could be together, like this, forever, I would say yes without even thinking. But..." I hesitated, sensing we were on the edge of everything. "You said at the distillery that you didn't want me turned, that you love me as I am."

"I never want to lose you," he breathed. "But losing you by death...at least it's honest. Real. Natural. If you became one of us, it would take longer, but I would eventually lose you in a different and much more painful way."

"How do you mean?"

"You're special because of who and what you are now," he said, placing a hand on my chest. "Your vulnerability. Your flaws. Your pain. They are all what makes you beautiful. If you became like me, those things would fade."

"You still have those things."

"Not in the same way you do," he said. "And I'm not even sure they're remnants of my human self. In you, they are what *makes* you human — and they would go. Not straight away... It would take years, perhaps hundreds of years, but it would happen. And I don't think I could survive watching that happen to you, watching you become someone else, lose everything that makes you who you are now."

"I don't want to change anything," I whispered. "This is what I want. *This*. What we have now, for as long as we have it. But..." With an almost inhuman effort, I made myself continue. "You are right. One day I will die. I don't know how to ask you to stay with me, knowing that you'll have to live through that."

He stared at the ring for a long time. I was certain, then, that this was the end. He would go. Now. Tonight. After having told me the truth, there was no way he could stay — nor could I let him, knowing that one day we would both be divided forever and he would have to carry on alone.

A whirling void opened in my gut as I prepared myself to say goodbye. But then he lifted my left hand, slipped the ring on my fourth finger and brought the hand to his lips. He kissed the knuckles, then took both my hands and held them to his chest. The storm in his eyes had settled and the usually sharp lines of his face had softened.

"We'll just have to spend your lifetime making enough memories to keep me going for mine," he said. Then he kissed me again.

It felt like that kiss could last forever, but I broke it long enough to catch a breath so I could say, "We need to get you a ring too."

He smiled openly. "You choose one for me," he said.

"I've had one picked out for ages," I admitted.

He laughed softly, though his eyes were still bright with tears, then I kissed him again, telling him everything that words couldn't sat.

The heat grew between us and we sank into the heather. Our breathing grew heavy, our touches more urgent. Terje's cool skin warmed to my touch. He brought me close then lifted his finger to my lips. The smell of the of red-black Blood on the pad filled my head and dizzied me with promise, but I pushed it back.

"No," I said, shaking my head. "I want to be human for you for as long as I can be."

We made love in the fragrant, dew-dropped heather with the stars shining over us and Glenroe glowing below, and I knew, then, that I would live forever in his heart.

Want to see more from this author?
Here's a taster for you to enjoy!

Sun, Sea and Small-Town Secrets
S. J. Coles

Excerpt

I turned over with a sigh. I'd thought that second bottle of red would help me sleep this time, but all I'd achieved was insomnia with a headache.

The moonlight creeping in round the edge of the blind illuminated the bold, minimalist prints on the walls and the simple, spartan furniture that was so at odds with the balmy, luscious countryside outside.

Gerrard had always liked his surroundings... controlled. Even the washing powder was the same brand he'd used in the flat at home, so the sheets smelled like him.

I pushed them back with a frustrated grumble then wandered into the living area. I stared at the open laptop on the desk, the piles of journals and drifts of paper surrounding it. I shook my head, returned to the bedroom, dressed then left the villa.

The cool night air felt good against my flushed skin. I strode along the seafront boulevard where the cafe and boulangerie shopfronts were bleached shades of grey in the moonlight. I took deep breaths, inhaling the smells of salt and dried seaweed.

I checked my phone. It was getting on for two-thirty. I rubbed my face, admitting I wasn't feeling much better than when I'd left the villa — no better than when I'd stepped off the plane a week before, either. I sat on a bench and gazed out over the deserted beach. During the day, the sand was so light and the sea so blue that it was almost tropical. Even at night it was beautiful, all shifting shadows and pale sand under a sky so vast and crowded with stars that it was like it belonged to another world.

I'd never visited France before. Hell, I'd never ventured outside the UK, apart from that one — and best forgotten — trip to Majorca with Gerrard for our anniversary. But I had to admit that Ruéier was picture-postcard perfect — small, unspoiled, off the beaten track, so not overrun by tourists and the inevitable high-street chains that followed them. It was everything Gerrard had said it was — the perfect place to get some distance and write my book.

So why can't I sleep?

I stood, thinking to walk the long way home and avoid analysing the question too deeply but stopped when the sound of voices rippled the easy quiet of the night. Stepping out from the shadow of a tree, I saw one of the boats in the harbour had its cabin light on. It illuminated the wide deck and a tall wheelhouse. Several figures were aboard and another on the pier, loading large bags into the hold.

I wasn't sure what made me look closer. There had to be plenty of reasons for loading a boat at night. But something about the way they moved and the low urgency of their muttered French raised the hairs on the back of my arms.

When the figure on the pier handed over the last heavy-looking holdall, his jacket lifted and I glimpsed a gun tucked in his waistband.

I stepped back into the shadows just as the hooded face turned my way. I held my breath. The voices went quiet but then the roar of the boat's engine tore through the silence.

I swore silently to myself. I'd come to Ruéier to get *away* from suspicious figures with guns. I held my breath for several more heartbeats before daring another look. The boat was heading for the harbour mouth and the figure from the pier was coming up the stairs less than five meters away. I ducked behind the tree and held still. I could hear his footsteps now, coming right for me.

He walked right past, heading south, down the boulevard toward the ferry port. His shoulders were hunched, his hands in his pockets and his head moved left to right as he scanned the shadows on either side.

I didn't breathe again until he'd turned a corner and disappeared.

* * * *

I woke the next morning, groggy and with a foul taste in my mouth. I moaned as I eased myself from the sofa, then groaned again when I saw the empty wine bottles on the coffee table. My head pounded. My stomach churned. And none of the memories, either those from the night before or the more painful ones from home, were any duller. I was now just hurting and hungover…again

Smart move, Seb.

I muttered to myself, shambled through the open-plan kitchen-dining area to the bedroom, avoiding tripping over the clothes scattered all over the floor, stripped and got into the shower.

When I was clean, dressed and in some semblance of order, I set the coffee machine going then sat at my laptop and began searching for the number for the local police force, silently berating myself for choosing to drink rather than deal with this mess the night before.

I sipped my brimming mug and tapped the number into my phone then hesitated. What exactly was I going to say? I was out in the middle of the night, on the wrong side of a couple of bottles and saw people getting onto a boat? Sure, I'd registered suspicious behaviour flags, but would the local *gendarmerie* care about my analytical body language profiles? The British police certainly hadn't.

I ground my teeth.

There was the gun, of course... *I did see a gun, right?* I rubbed my eyes, trying to remember. Had there been guns? Or was I just channelling memories I seemed to be having trouble leaving behind?

While I was musing on this, an email popped in from my publisher.

Dear Mr. Conway,
It has been several weeks since we received your proposal. We would very much like to assess your progress on the project so far.
Kind regards.

I blanched, forgetting all about the boat, hurriedly opened all my draft files and forced my bleary mind to engage.

I made myself work all day. That was what I was here for, I reminded myself. And Daisy was counting on me.

By lunch, I was physically recovered enough to open more wine and eat bread and cheese with one hand whilst typing with the other. As evening began to creep in, I finally found myself with a structure plan and two opening Chapters that I thought were heading somewhere. I took a breath, wrote a brief email to the publisher then sent it all off.

I opened another bottle just as there was a knock on the door.

I glanced at the clock on the wall, frowning. It was getting on for eight p.m. and the cleaner, the only visitor I had, wasn't due until the next day.

The knocking came again, more insistently.

"Monsieur Conway?"

The voice was muffled by the wood, but the words were distinct. I muttered to myself, put my glass aside, opened the door and promptly stopped breathing.

The man standing on the doorstep wasn't someone who would normally take my breath away. He was tall, sure and his shoulders broad, like I liked. But his suit was dull, unfashionable and did not fit well. The washed-out grey did not complement his sun-warmed complexion and his fair hair was cut short, a functional style that, to me, looked like a quick fix for the slight curl.

His jaw was firm but not chiselled. He was clean-shaven, his lips thin and without expression—and the man was also, undoubtedly, law enforcement. It was obvious from the way he stood, the way he took me in, assessing every detail—middle grade, no one special, too old to be on his way up, too young to be on his way out.

But it wasn't that which had the blood rushing through my body. It was his eyes. They were the deep, dark grey of a storm cloud, a colour I'd never seen in human eyes before. I was normally so good at reading people—or at least able to recognise when they were hiding something, which people nearly always are. But these eyes were so open, so expressive and so...*charged* that it caused my heart to clench in my chest. It was like looking out to sea on a stormy night, all beauty, wonder and natural forces clashing, with a dash of danger mixed in.

"Monsieur?"

I cleared my throat and nodded. "Yes, how can I help?"

"English, yes?" he said, his accent swaying around the words like waves rolling along the shore.

I hurriedly suppressed the thought. "That's right."

He produced a badge. "*Gendarme* Antoine Damboise, *Gendarmerie Nationale*...and my superior, *Adjudant* Delphine Rayne." A woman in a smarter suit but with a grimmer expression joined him on the step, examining me keenly thorough thin-rimmed glasses. He murmured a few words to her in French, and she nodded and gestured for him to continue. "We are the police."

"Yes, I know what the *gendarmerie* is. What do you want with me?"

"We would like to ask you a couple of questions, if we may."

"What about?"

Damboise smiled slightly—a pleasant expression, though it didn't brighten the darkness in his eyes. "Can we come in, Monsieur?"

Rayne watched me closely as I showed them into the living room. They took in the desk scattered with books and papers, a half-drank mug off coffee next to the laptop and the open bottle of wine next to that.

I retrieved my glass and moved to top it up, feeling their stares on my back.

"So, what's this about?"

Rayne murmured more French and Damboise asked, "Are you here on holiday, Monsieur?"

"No. Well, yes. Well…no…"

"Which?" Rayne asked, her accent thicker than Damboise, the word weighted more carefully and harder in tone.

"I'm here to work," I said, gesturing at the desk. "But not my…usual work."

"What is your usual work?" Damboise again.

"I work for a private medical practice," I hedged.

"Doctor?" Rayne asked.

"Not clinical, no…"

Damboise translated for her, and she nodded. "What is *this* work?" she said, nodding at the desk.

"I'm writing a book."

"Ah, you're an author?" Damboise said, pulling a notepad and pen from his pocket.

"An academic," I said, shutting the laptop with a click as the detective attempted to read the screen.

"You came to Ruéier to write a book?"

"Is that so hard to believe?"

Damboise shrugged, examining his notebook. "Our holiday makers are usually…older. Here for the sea, the quiet."

"I need quiet too."

Damboise scribbled more notes. "Have you been here before? Maybe writing other books?"

"No," I said, impatience beginning to sharpen my words. "This is my first time…first book."

Rayne asked something in French, and Damboise translated whilst watching me closely. "And what made you choose Ruéier, Monsieur?"

"Look… I don't know what this is—"

"Please, just answer the question."

I sighed. "It was recommended by a friend. This is his villa."

"Who?" Rayne again.

"Why does that matter?"

"Maybe it does not," Damboise said in a conciliatory tone, glancing at Rayne, who pursed her lips. "And how long are you planning to stay?"

"I don't know, exactly."

"No return flight booked?" Damboise said carefully, his grey gaze on my face.

"I'll leave when the book's done. Am I in some sort of trouble?"

"We're just asking everyone in the area the same questions."

"Why?"

"There have been reports of some burglaries in the area. Holiday homes, mostly. Have you had any trouble?"

"Nothing here."

"You keep your doors and windows locked at night?"

"Of course."

"Forgive me…" Damboise had a dimple when he smiled. It transformed his face, making it appear almost boyish, though he must be approaching forty. I was not prepared for the thrumming it started in my nerves and hastily swallowed more wine. "It might seem like a silly question, but Ruéier is a quiet town. Some of our, how you say, 'older' people are not used to locking their doors."

"Times change, I guess."

"Quite correct," Damboise replied, regret weighting his words. "Unfortunate…but correct."

"Is that it?"

"Not quite." Damboise looked at Rayne, who swiped at her phone then showed me the screen.

"Have you seen this man, Monsieur?" she asked.

The man who glowered out of the photo was thin, pale and with a rough scruff along a jaw that was all hard lines and defiance. His hair was buzzed close to his head and there was a tribal tattoo on his neck. Something about his stance, the defiant set to his shoulders tickled at the back of my mind. But then nearly every criminal I'd ever known stood like that in their file photos — the guilty ones, anyway.

I shook my head. "No."

"You're sure?" Damboise asked.

"He's pretty distinctive. Is this your burglar?"

"We don't know who is behind the break-ins," Damboise said. "But this is a person of interest. You've not seen him around?"

"As I said, no."

Damboise nodded. "Have you seen anything else suspicious?"

I turned my back to fill my glass again. It was easier to focus when I couldn't see his eyes, but I still couldn't quite put my finger on what was making me so uneasy. *Damboise, certainly.* His unremarkable face was doing rather remarkable things to me that I really didn't have time for. *It must be the wine*, I said to myself — *that and the sexual frustration.* I took a breath and fought through nervousness snaking over my back and turned to face them again.

"Well…there is one thing."

"What?" Rayne asked.

"I thought I saw something odd at the harbour last night."

"At the 'arbour?" Rayne said.

"Le port," Damboise translated and Rayne's eyes hardened. "What did you see?" Damboise asked, his pen poised.

"I'm not sure," I said, taking a large mouthful of wine in an attempt to drown the prickling in my belly. "It's probably nothing."

"Monsieur, please," Damboise said, his expression intent. "Anything could be important."

I sat in the armchair, staring into the empty fireplace. "I saw a boat launch, which isn't that weird, I guess. But it was after two in the morning…"

Rayne asked something, frowning in a frustrated way. Damboise chattered back to her, and I caught the words *bateau* and *deux heures du matin.*

"Pêcheurs de nui," Rayne said with a dismissive wave of her hand. "Night fishermen," she said, slowly. "Many small boats fish in the night."

"It was a big boat," I said. "And these weren't fishermen."

"No?" Damboise sat on the edge of the sofa, elbows on his knees, looking at me intently. "How do you know?"

"The way they moved. The tone of their voices. Their clothes." I shrugged again. "They weren't going fishing."

Rayne muttered in French again, shaking her head.

"I know what I saw," I replied, hearing disbelief in her tone. "And, well…"

"Yes?" Damboise said.

I took a breath, my skin chilling all over again. "I think they had guns—or one of them did, at least."

Damboise pressed his lips together. "Are you sure?"

"It was dark," I said carefully, "but there was a light in the cabin. I was going to report it, but I wasn't sure— and I know you can get firearms licenses here. By the time I got back, I…" I trailed off, glancing at the line of empty wine bottles by the bin.

Damboise followed my glance without comment. "How many men were there?"

"Three, I think? Maybe four."

"How big was this boat?"

"Quite big…with a tall wheelhouse. I didn't see the colour or name."

"And these men? They launched this boat and, what? Took it out to sea?"

"That's right," I said, seeing it all playing out in front of my eyes again, the uneasiness returning. "Well, all except one."

"One?"

"Yes. One of them stayed behind."

"Where did he go?"

"He came right past me," I said, suppressing a shudder. "Up the boulevard, toward the ferry port."

"What did he look like? Where did he go?"

"I don't know… I was behind a tree."

"A tree?"

"One of the big acacias along the sea front," I said. "Outside the Café De La Mer?"

"Why were you outside so late, Monsieur?" Rayne put in.

"I couldn't sleep." I said, returning her look with a level one of my own.

"*Merci beaucoup*, Monsieur Conway," Damboise said, tucking his notebook back in his pocket. "Thank you very much. If it is possible, I would like you to come to the station tomorrow to make a more detailed statement."

Rayne chattered protests at him, and he replied calmly. She folded her arms and gave a stiff nod, then Damboise turned back to me. "Can you come?"

"You think they were dangerous?"

"We're not sure," he said, standing. "But an official statement would be helpful, if you please."

"Of course," I replied, also standing and taking the warm hand the detective offered. He had a firm grip, and his smile was pleasant, though his eyes seemed darker than before. "Anything I can do."

Damboise opened the door, and Rayne proceeded him out into the night.

"*Gendarme* Damboise?" I said, making a shoddy job at pronunciation and ignoring the voice in my head with long-practiced ease. He paused. "I can help you."

He raised his eyebrows. For one excruciating second, I thought he had guessed every inappropriate thought that had passed through my mind since he'd walked in the door, but I quashed any visible reaction.

"I often work with the police in the UK," I said, "as a profiler."

His eyebrows rose farther. "You're a, how you say, psychiatrist?"

"Psychologist," I corrected, a little archly, "with the West Midlands Police."

"That is a very gracious offer, Monsieur," he said, "but we could not involve a witness in an ongoing investigation."

"I'm good," I said. "And I know how to be discreet."

"Good to know." This time I was sure that there was something warmer in his expression, and my blood thrummed. "We shall see you tomorrow, Monsieur," he said, holding out a business card. "Around ten would be good, if you don't mind."

After he had gone, I downed the remainder of my wine and opened another bottle, shaking my head as I filled my glass nearly to the top. *What the hell am I doing?* I wasn't there to flirt with strangely attractive French policemen…even if he did stir something in me that had been dormant for a long time.

I swallowed some wine the wrong way then spent the next few minutes spluttering and coughing until my lungs were clear. With a string of curses, I grudgingly put the bottle back in the fridge. This was classic rebound behaviour — not that there was anything wrong with a no-strings fuck whilst getting my head round the consequential parts of life. But someone like Damboise was all strings.

That didn't stop me from thinking about what he might look like under that shapeless suit as I climbed between the sheets.

PUBLISHING

Sign up for our newsletter and find out about all our
romance book releases, eBook sales and promotions,
sneak peeks and FREE romance books!

About the Author

S. J. Coles is a Romance writer originally from Shropshire, UK. She has been writing stories for as long as she has been able to read them. Her biggest passion is exploring narratives through character relationships.

She finds writing LGBT/paranormal romance provides many unique and fulfilling opportunities to explore many (often neglected or under-represented) aspects of human experience, expectation, emotion and sexuality.

Among her biggest influences are LGBT Romance authors K J Charles and Josh Lanyon and Vampire Chronicles author Anne Rice.

J. J. Coles loves to hear from readers. You can find her contact information, website details and author profile page at https://www.pride-publishing.com